BACK HOME
FOR LOVE

Indiana Romance 5

I0554583

Leanne Malloy

Back Home For Love
Leanne Malloy

Paperback Edition

Published in the United States by
Wolfpack Publishing, Las Vegas

CKN Christian Publishing
An Imprint of Wolfpack Publishing
5130 S. Fort Apache Road 215-380
Las Vegas, NV 89148

cknchristianpublishing.com

Paperback ISBN: 978-1-63977-305-3
eBook ISBN: 978-1-63977-307-7

Library of Congress Catalog Number: 2022942078

BACK HOME
FOR LOVE

For Bill – my husband, best friend, and partner in life. Thanks for your loving care this past year, and always!

Prologue

As the cheerful restaurant noise surrounded them, Kaye Anderson reflected on the beautiful wedding they'd just attended. Courtney and Greg were so much in love it oozed out of their pores. Their families were proud and grateful for the marriage of two good souls. She sipped her iced tea and studied her second daughter. Katie looked good, better than she had in a while. Ending her relationship with the respiratory therapist had been a good move. While Dan was nice, Kaye knew Katie well enough to realize he was no match for the young woman's fiery passion for life. Dan was steady, hardworking, and even-tempered, but he was simply not what her daughter required for happiness. Katie needed someone with a temperament to equal hers. Dan was just a little bland.

"What is it, Mom?" Katie asked. "You've got something on your mind."

Knowing better than to mention Dan, Kaye shifted her thoughts. "I do, Katie. As I said before the wedding, I want to talk about my plans. I'll be honest. Moving to Phoenix was not my best decision."

"Okaaay," Katie drawled. "I'll admit, I'm not surprised. You've been hinting at this for a while. Where are you headed now?"

"Somewhere without unrelenting heat. Somewhere with traffic that a woman can get through without elevating her blood pressure to stroke level. And a place with friends who know my history and my likes and dislikes, without my having to reintroduce myself all the time." Kaye sipped her drink again and wondered what Katie's reaction would be.

"Mom, you don't want to move back to Gordon, do you? After all your complaining about wanting to avoid winter and the agony of small-town living? You can't be serious," Katie said. She looked at her mother and shook her head.

"I know, I know," Kaye replied. "But it was a decision made in the throes of grief for your father. And, yes, I've always hated winter. Who knew I'd hate temperatures of one hundred fifteen degrees even more? If one more person says, 'But it's a *dry* heat,' I'll strangle them."

Katie laughed. "I agree, Mom. Phoenix is a good place, but I've decided it's not a permanent spot for me either. That said, I doubt Gordon is my destination. Maybe Indianapolis, or Knoxville, or somewhere on the coast like Charleston." She twisted the wrapper from her straw and looked at her mother. "And then there's my job. I'll need a transfer with my company or a different position with a place anxious for a newly minted MBA. Just the thought of a job search makes me tired."

"Yes, it's tough to know for sure," Kaye replied. "You have to do you, as the young folks say. But I'm headed back to Indiana."

"We have an early flight tomorrow," Katie noted. "We need to be at the airport by five-thirty in the morning, and then pray our connection in Charlotte is on time and doesn't lose our luggage. We can discuss this when we're back in Arizona." She sighed, looking dejected. "When we're not so homesick after seeing the people from Indiana here at the wedding."

The pair left their table and headed back to their hotel room. They forced themselves to pack and set double alarms to ensure they'd awaken on time. As she eased herself into one of the queen-sized beds, Kaye turned to her daughter. "Katie, you'd find a job in no time. And if the insurance industry isn't for you, there are lots of other options. Don't sell yourself short."

Katie Anderson burrowed under her bed's cozy covers and marveled at her mother's desire to leave Phoenix. At the same time, she understood her mom's rationale. Katie was tired of the stress of her job and of the gigantic metro area comprising greater Phoenix. Sure, there were tons of things to do, lots of cultural opportunities, and a lack of freezing winter weather. But that last thing made Christmas sort of a sham. Katie missed snow and ice, of all things. She missed going to the summer downtown farmers markets without driving fifty minutes to get to them. She missed holiday shopping for her childhood friends, whose tastes she knew from years of being besties.

If she were honest, she'd also begun to hate her job. Despite her MBA, she was still a glorified insurance clerk, doing the grunt tasks of claims work while simultaneously manning the desk at the front door of the tiny branch office in suburban Chandler, Arizona. Her daily commute had her tallying the hours she wasted on the road. Audiobooks were helpful, but she had to concentrate on the congested traffic and would often miss important plot points as a result. She disliked admitting it, but her mother's points were valid. She'd been thinking similarly for several months.

The tipping point, though, had been her sister Kristen's revelation at the wedding reception that Gordon Community College was looking for an MBA grad to direct the new business internship program. The job description seemed to be an ideal fit for Katie. It required work experience, a knowledge of business opportunities in Gordon and central Indiana, and an interest in teaching one course per semester. That description had been written for Katie Anderson.

Dan had made a potential move easy, too. He'd been ready to take their relationship to the "next level." Katie's reaction had been telling, most of all to her. She had almost visibly recoiled, suddenly filled with the realization that a life with Dan would be as stifling as the Arizona heat.

Meeting for lunch the Saturday after they returned to Phoenix, the Anderson women resumed their discussion of a possible move. In Kaye's world, the move had shifted from possible to inevitable.

"Honey, I've given my notice to the apartment staff here and scheduled a truck for the first of next month. And I've reserved a two-bedroom cottage at Gordon Park. It's a gorgeous new subdivision thirty minutes outside of town, just off I-70. I love the concept; the planners have built a mix of traditional single-family homes, townhouses, and a gated section with cottages limited to those of us over fifty-five. What do you think?"

Katie thought her mother might be going through one of her famed impetuous periods. She was careful, though. "Mom, this is very sudden. Are you sure? Maybe you should wait until after the first of March so you can avoid another Indiana winter before you move. What's the rush?"

"No rush, I'm just ready," Kaye replied. "You don't need to worry. It's not as sudden as you think. I've been planning this for six months. Kristen's new baby was probably the trigger. Courtney's wedding cinched it for me."

Kaye munched on her salad. After a healthy bite of Caesar-drenched chicken and parmesan, she continued, "As I watched all the people from Gordon at the reception, I realized how much I missed everyone, including those who used to get under my skin. Even Rose Dolce, with her unending advice, had appeal. I'm ready, Katie. It will be fine. What about you?"

"I may be more ready than you think, Mom. We'll see."

Chapter One

Kaye marveled at the joy her new little cottage brought her. The twelve-hundred-square-foot abode was perfect for her needs. Bigger than her apartment in Phoenix, but still manageable. Plus, her yard work and snow removal were included in a reasonable HOA fee. She thanked God and her late husband, Stan, for the financial freedom she possessed. So many of those she knew were barely making it on their Social Security payments.

She had decorated her bedroom with furniture she and Stan bought years ago. The carved wood set was dated but had classic lines and was full of sweet memories. New bedding and wall art updated the decor just enough. The second bedroom was a combination guest room and office. Thanking God again, this time for discount big-box stores, she had purchased a full-sized bed and small desk with an upholstered chair. The look was more modern than her main bedroom, but still held Kaye's imprint with a wall of family photos and a wedding ring quilt on the bed made decades past by her mother.

Feeling proud of her work, she was debating the purchase of new dinnerware (several current plates and mugs had been chipped in the move, damage she was secretly happy about) when her doorbell rang. Tickled that she was about to have her first visitor, she answered eagerly.

Standing on her porch was the last person she expected or wanted to see. Bob Benson, GCC scum and vindictive power player. Kaye made no attempt to be civil.

"Bob Benson. What could you possibly be doing here?"

He had the grace to look humble. "Hello, Kaye. I'm here to welcome you to Gordon Park. As president of our over fifty-five resident association, I let new owners know about our many clubs and activities."

Kaye stood rigid and silent.

Bob tried again. "I want to apologize again for my indiscretion a few years ago. I asked you out because you're an attractive, vibrant woman. Your husband's recent passing was lost on me/ I'd just heard you were a widow, nothing more."

Squinting, Kaye took a deep breath. "Sure, Bob. And my refusal to go out with you had nothing to do with your treatment of my daughter Kristen? She had to forfeit her full-time role at GCC for a whole semester thanks to your trumped-up accusations of her mistreating a student. It seems to me your 'indiscretion' amounts to more than not realizing I was a new widow."

"True," Bob said with a wince. "For what it's worth, I was in a bad spot myself. My wife had died suddenly the year before. My actions were inexcusable but came from a place of real pain. I did everything in my power to make it up to Kristen before I retired last year."

This was true, Kaye thought. Kristen had filled her in about Bob's generous letter when she applied for a promotion, and also about his support of her grant applications. But still. He wasn't going to get off easy from this protective mama bear.

"Whatever," Kaye said. "So why are you here again?"

"I usually meet with new residents and give them this booklet that details our many opportunities for social activities, trips, and so on. May I come in so we can talk about all of it?"

Kaye took the booklet from him and shut the door. There was no way she would allow this sociopath in her home. Peering through the peephole, she saw Bob shrug and walk away. Good riddance.

As she put Bob out of her mind and continued her mental debate about what kind of new dishes to buy, her phone jangled with her older daughter's distinctive ring tone. Kristen always seemed to have radar about her mother's mental turmoil. Kaye smiled and answered.

"Hi there, Kristen," she said. "What's going on?"

"Not much, Mom. I wanted to ask if you'd be up for a walk on your new property grounds with me and Bernie. He's always enthused to explore new places and he needs the stimulation."

Kristen's goldendoodle was still mostly a puppy despite being five years old. She added, "Of course, I'll bring the baby, too. She enjoys a good stroller ride with Grandma."

"I'd love to see little Michelle. And Bernie, too. Come on over."

"You okay, Mom? You sound tense." Kristen's psychologist radar was still intact.

"I'm fine, dear. I'll tell you about the latest when you get here."

Kristen arrived with Bernie, Michelle, and the usual plethora of baby gear in tow. Kaye wondered how she'd managed to raise two girls without all the latest gadgets and gizmos. Baby wipe warmers! Strollers that turned into car seats! Homemade, organic, steamed baby foods! Gerber had sure saved her a lot of time and money back in the day, as had nonorganic, heavily sweetened cereal. Smiling at her granddaughter, she helped Kristen unload.

After smothering Michelle with kisses and dutifully patting Bernie, Kaye pushed the stroller. Kristen took the dog leash as they began their walk. Michelle commented on the beautiful grounds with baby gibberish and then began to settle. Soon she was asleep.

"Fill me in, Mom," Kristen said. "Something's got you rattled."

"You'll never guess who's the president of the old-timer's association here," Kaye muttered. "Just when I thought this place was perfect."

"No clue."

"Bob Benson! He had the nerve to come over uninvited with his supposed welcome packet."

Kristen paused, obviously searching for a diplomatic response. After checking on the baby, she said, "I understand that Bob must bring back a lot of painful memories, Mom. Dad had just died and then Bob hurt me professionally in revenge for your unwillingness to date him. But I believe he's a better person now. He's helped me a lot at GCC. I even spoke for him at his retirement party."

"You did? I can't imagine, Kristen."

"Yes, I did. Mom, you're the one always talking about God's help and forgiveness. Can't you believe that Bob could change?" She stopped while Bernie squatted to do his business and then cleaned up after him. "And I saw Bob's devastation after his wife died. The man was truly in love. They'd been married longer than you and Dad. It took him a long time to recover."

"Maybe. I do believe people can change and all that, but Bob was so creepy. And he damaged your career. It took you an extra year to get promoted."

"Yes, but I was newly married and adjusting to being a stepmother, so the extra time without the promotion application pressure was a back-door blessing. And Bob was the most fervent supporter of my application. My department chair said she'd never read a more positive letter from him."

Kaye was silent. Everything Kristen said was valid. It just seemed wrong to let Bob off the hook after such mean-spirited actions. Even now, the memory of that time in her life caused a physical ache in her chest. Forgiveness, she knew, would help her as much as Bob. But she wasn't ready.

After their walk, Bernie settled in on Kaye's sofa while Kristen fed Michelle. The pureed plums looked lovely, but somehow not worth the effort of steaming, peeling, and processing them. Then again, Kristen was a fantastic mother, and it was none of Kaye's business how she fed Michelle. As she fixed their lunch (homemade chicken salad with yogurt dressing in honor of Kristen's healthy eating), she brought up a different topic. She was done talking about Bob.

"How's Sophie? When will she stay with you next?"

Sophie, Kristen's stepdaughter from Indianapolis, was a lively ten-year-old. Kristen smiled and shrugged. "She'll be here for two weeks at the end of September. The balanced schedule that her school district uses allows for longer vacation periods."

Kaye noted the shrug and probed further. "Are you good with that? Any problems with Sophie?"

"No real problems," Kristen said. "She's in a new phase, though. Ten-year-old kids are much more advanced than when I was at that age. Sophie talks constantly about clothes and is nagging Mike about getting a cell phone. So far, he and Anita are united that Sophie's too young for that."

Kaye hugged her daughter, understanding more than Kristen was willing to say. Anita, Mike's first wife and Sophie's mother, was for the most part a fine woman. She and Mike were good parents to Sophie, and since they both had another child by their current spouses, the relationship triangle maintained a fine but delicate balance. Kristen was often in the middle, even when conflicts weren't a factor.

"It's probably a tough call, though I can barely tolerate my phone. I need it to function, but technology has so many glitches I want to pull my hair out some days." Kaye dished up their sandwiches and added some freshly cut fruit. "My experience aside, there are pros and cons both ways. Some say kids need phones given the violence in schools. On the other hand, bullying on social media is a real risk."

"Exactly, Mom!" Kristen exclaimed. "Mike only sees the safety side of the argument. I deal with kids on the receiving end of nasty social media comments. It can be truly traumatizing."

Kaye studied Kristen, knowing more was going on. "Not an easy decision. How are you and Mike handling it?"

"Fine, I guess. Mike still wants to be the cool dad with Sophie. He'll figure it out, though. And she's not my daughter."

Now Kaye understood. "Who's telling you that? Sophie? Anita? Mike?"

After only a few bites of her sandwich, Kristen blinked, stood, and began to gather her things to go. "I'm going to scoot, Mom. Michelle will be fussy if she wakes up without her blanket, which I left on the kitchen counter." She stopped and hugged Kaye fiercely. "Thanks for listening, Mom. And double thanks for figuring out what was bothering me. As usual, you're right on target. I'm not Sophie's mom, but I get to 'mother' her several weeks a year."

Kaye gave Kristen's departing form a gentle wave. Mike and Kristen were brilliant people. Sophie wouldn't come between them. Time would help them solve this latest tween dilemma. But she ached for her daughter's pain. Who said having grown kids was a breeze?

After two weeks in her new home, Kaye had almost all the finishing touches completed. Her new dishes were a bargain find from a home supply store. Towels in the latest designer shades complemented her two bathrooms. She had even laid an area rug in the living room, scooting the sofa around with furniture sliders under each leg. Kaye was proud of her work. Her reward would be some quality reading and quiet time.

The doorbell rang just as she was sipping a soft drink and reading the jacket blurb from the latest novel by her favorite author. She was happy to see her neighbor, Linda, on the porch. Like Kaye, Linda was a widow adjusting to being alone.

"Come in, come in!" Kaye said. "I'm happy you're here, Linda."

"I'm not interrupting anything?"

"No, just some quiet time, which I have plenty of. What's new with you?"

"Same old stuff," Linda said. She sipped the bubbled water Kaye had provided and continued, "Are you going to join any clubs, Kaye? There are so many to choose from. I've decided on the book club and the walking group."

"Walking sounds good," Kaye answered. "I've been lax about getting my steps in since I moved here. And I love to read. What kind of books does the club focus on?"

"Mostly chick-lit novels. Occasionally we branch out with cozy mysteries. There's another group for current nonfiction, but I don't care to rehash the evening news with folks who are my neighbors. Too many differences of political opinion," Linda said with a knowing look.

"Got it," Kaye said. "And I'll meet you the next time you walk."

"Tomorrow at seven," Linda said with a wink. "We start early, no matter what season we're in. Some of the members are still working, others watch their grandkids, and most everyone else is booked for appointments throughout the day."

Kaye smiled and the two enjoyed other topics for

the rest of the visit. After Linda left, Kaye put her book aside. She had to pick out some comfortable walking clothes.

Indiana weather cooperated as usual the next morning, meaning it did not cooperate at all. The steady drizzle was heavy enough to make Kaye grateful for her baseball cap and raincoat. She turned the corner to the starting point Linda had indicated and was surprised to see only one person. His back was to her, but Kaye knew who he was. The dreary day became even more frustrating. Bob Benson was a member of the walker's club. The only faithful member from the looks of things.

He turned to her as Kaye was considering ducking behind a parked car so she wouldn't be seen. "Ah, Kaye. I was hoping you'd join us today," he said.

"Here I am," she said. "Should we cancel the walk? The weather is awful and there's just the two of us."

"No, let's proceed," Bob said with a grin. "The weather station said the drizzle is almost finished. Are you game?"

Irritated by his implied challenge, Kaye gave Bob her sweetest, fakest, smile. "Sure am."

They walked at a comfortable pace, with Bob pointing out various landmarks of their housing development. He was also an expert on trees, the few flowers still around, and the grassy berms that provided some privacy between the backs of the newly built homes. In spite of herself, Kaye listened carefully and was forced to engage.

"All the scenery aside, Bob, what made you move to Gordon Park? My story is obvious. I missed Gordon and all the people."

"After my wife died, I couldn't imagine leaving our home. It was full of comforting memories, and our kids liked coming back for holidays. But it's been a few years now, and the big house was becoming a burden. Both in terms of cleaning and upkeep and with all the things that reminded me of the past. What had been comforting was becoming depressing. So, last Christmas I told the kids what I was going through. I was shocked at their kindness and empathy for my feelings. We had a big gathering at the start of the summer. They each took the things that meant most to them and we had an auction for the rest. Long story short, I built a cottage at Gordon Park. It's been a good change for me. How's it going for you?"

Kaye studied the man at her side. His story seemed genuine. Kristen said he'd changed. She had nothing to lose by confiding in him, so she did. "My story is less cohesive than yours. Stan died and I went a little nuts. I was convinced that a move to Phoenix, where my daughter Katie lived, would make me whole. I was sure a warm climate and a fresh start would fix it all."

Bob smiled in understanding and she continued, "You can predict the rest. I needed to grieve. I underestimated how hot Arizona gets. Turns out snow is not all that bad."

Bob threw his head back and laughed. "Especially since we're not working!" Bob said. "If the weather's bad, I have a third cup of coffee and thank the good Lord I don't have to deal with icy streets and slick sidewalks to get into my office."

"True. But the warm weather was nice for my

joints," Kaye added. "Listen to me, Bob! I'm talking like a true old lady...soon you'll be hearing about the merits of heating pads versus ice packs. I'm sorry to be so boring."

They laughed in unison and were soon back at their starting point.

"That's two miles in, Kaye. Some of the walkers log their distances. Now you know the distance today's path covered. Will you be walking again with us?"

"Sure, I will," Kaye stated. "Next time there should be more of us, right? You won't be subjected to my dreary conversation."

"Not dreary at all, Kaye. I enjoyed it immensely."

Kaye walked slowly back to her home. She'd planned to blister Bob in front of the other walkers today. It had seemed important to let others know what kind of person he was. But either God or Kristen had helped her begin the forgiveness journey. It felt good. She still didn't trust Bob Benson, but she understood him better. He'd been kind to her as well. Maybe she'd needed forgiving, too, after the way she'd treated him when he'd visited with the literature describing all Gordon Park had to offer.

Disliking herself even more, she wondered about how she'd looked. Bob had been very dapper in his knee-length trench coat. In contrast, her Cubs baseball cap and old yoga pants were somewhat dreary. She also questioned her decision to let her hair grow into its natural color. Wasn't the gray look trendy? It might be, but she couldn't hide her sixty-seven years very well when she had salt-and-pepper locks. At least it had kept its natural curl. And her skin was okay.

What was going on with her? Her ruminations sounded like those of a teenage girl! She hadn't compared herself to younger women in a while. Surely Bob wasn't the source of such self-doubt. No, she simply wanted to look and be her best, no matter what her age.

The stress of the move back to Indiana had resulted in ten extra pounds to boot. It made little sense to diet now, with the fall season kicking off the best eating of the year. She would diet starting in January. That's what New Year's resolutions were for anyway. Maybe she'd even keep a food journal or use a snazzy app on her phone to track calories and exercise. She laughed out loud, knowing better. Who said writing down her food was a good idea? That young doctor in Phoenix had been a fan of that approach, but Kaye always lasted two days, max. She wasn't a calorie accountant, she just wanted to live a good life!

As she put away her jacket, she heard a knock at the front door. Odd that someone didn't use the bell. She opened the door and was surprised to see Linda. A very tearful Linda.

"What's wrong, honey? Come on in." Kaye held the door while simultaneously hugging her new friend.

"I'm a mess, as usual," Linda said. "When I asked you to walk with us today, I forgot it was the anniversary of my husband's death."

"Understandable," Kaye said softly.

"No, it's not what you think. I'm pretty much at peace with Max's passing. It's that I'm alone and afraid I always will be. I loved being married. Max and I built a good life. We were best friends. I want all that again. But the odds are terrible, right? This place is full of single women. The few available men know their status and can be awful." She sniffed loudly and wiped her eyes again.

"This sounds familiar," Kaye answered. "At my old complex in Phoenix, the widowed and single men were treated like royalty by some of the women. It was almost laughable. I also understand what you mean about being alone. I enjoy my independence sometimes, but there's a void. Female friends are wonderful, but male companionship would be nice."

Kaye served them the last of the fruit salad she'd made for Kristen and continued. "Anything else bothering you?"

"It's that Bob Benson," Linda admitted. "He's just adorable, don't you think? I've had him over for dinner, suggested that we visit some fall festivals together, and on and on. He's sweet but won't accept any more of my invitations. I think I have a school-girl crush on him, Kaye! As I said, I'm a mess."

Kaye grinned at Linda. "You're not a mess. You're lonely, and according to my psychologist daughter who thinks she knows everything, loneliness can be pretty painful. Bob's okay, but he's not Harrison Ford, after all. Your judgment is skewed, pal."

They laughed and Kaye broke out the package of gourmet pumpkin spice cookies she'd been saving for a special occasion. "Calories be damned," she said to Linda. "We're worth a little treat."

Linda left after an hour, and Kaye cleaned up her dining area. She couldn't believe it. Bob Benson was the local heartthrob. He may have been nice to her today, but she doubted he could be counted on to continue. His ugly treatment of Kristen was a fact, despite all his explanations and attempts to make nice. And after all, he was Gordon Park's resident hunk!

Chapter Two

Katie Anderson looked at her newly minted campus ID badge. She'd taken a decent picture for a change. Hopefully it was a good omen for her new job as director of business internships at Gordon Community College. Her first few weeks had gone well. She had made inroads with faculty members, a process helped tremendously by Kristen. Her sister was an established faculty member and most remembered her as Kristen Anderson, not Kristen Sutliff. That was fine with Katie. She'd take all the help she could get. Kristen had even enlisted the aid of Annie Dolce Upton, whose nursing students didn't need internships, since they trained at clinical settings approved by their program. But like Kristen, Annie had lots of campus contacts. To Annie's further credit, she'd made the point to her colleagues that "business" internships weren't solely for business majors. Most professions had some component of dollars-and-cents tracking. As of yesterday, Katie had matched twice the number of student/internship pairings than her initial goal. So far, so good.

After she finished her monthly report to her dean, Katie shut down her laptop and watered the succulent plant holding pride of place in her office. Given her brown thumb, her mother had gifted her with the hearty plant both to congratulate her on her new job and to remind them of their shared time in Phoenix. Neither of them had any regrets. Living in Gordon, Indiana, was a welcome change.

As she was walking to her car, her cell phone rang. Kristen's voice sounded tired and stressed. "Hey, Katie. I need help tonight." Kristen shifted the phone to her alternate ear, a sign she had baby Michelle on her hip. "Mike has a late shift at the hospital, and I forgot I need to attend a Psych Club dinner meeting on campus. Sophie insists she can watch Michelle, but I doubt she's ready. Is there any way you could come by? I'll provide pizza and salad."

Katie had learned to measure Kristen's desperation by the quality of pizza. "What kind of pie are we talking about, Sis?"

"Well, you know thin crust is better for you, and the veggie supreme has all your vegetable servings for the day. Will that work?"

"It will not," Katie teased. "I will need a three-meat deep-dish pan pizza, with garlic bread sticks. Sophie will like that better anyway."

"Fine," Kristen said, defeated. "But you'd be surprised at what Sophie likes and dislikes these days. You'll see."

Wondering what Kristen meant, Katie headed home. Her newly purchased rambler was her pride and joy. Furnishings from her apartment in Phoenix looked lovely against the classic lines of her 1950s one-story house. Pops of color dominated the "public" spaces, with pillows, abstract art, and lamps tying it all together. Her three tiny bedrooms were more sparsely furnished, which was fine with her. All she needed in her room was a bed and table lamp to read by. The rest would come later.

Since Kristen and Mike lived only five minutes away, Katie arrived soon after the call. Kristen met her at the door.

"The pizza and breadsticks are on their way," Kristen said. "Michelle's been fed and will be happy to be with you and Sophie until her bedtime at eight. I'll be home by nine. Call if anything comes up."

"You're welcome," Katie muttered as she looked at Kristen's departing backside. Entering the house, she called out a greeting to Sophie. "Sophie Sutliff, where are you? We haven't seen each other in ages."

Michelle grinned her semi-toothless greeting from her swing in the formal living room as Katie looked for Sophie. She found the young girl in the family room, watching television. "Hey, you. Long time no see."

Sophie gave her a shaded glare. "Yeah, it's been a while, Aunt Katie."

Great. After a full day at work, I get to play games with a sullen ten-year-old. Or was Sophie eleven? Didn't matter. She was rude and clearly upset about something. The doorbell rang and Katie retrieved the pizza order. "We've got food, Soph. It smells divine. Come on over and we'll eat while we give Michelle bits of crust."

"Not hungry," Sophie yelled. "I just had a bag of chips and some chocolate chip cookies."

What? The world's healthiest couple was allowing Sophie to eat chips and cookies as dinner? Well,

Mike wasn't here, which meant Kristen had caved to Sophie's mood and allowed her a junk-food meal. Which was probably no big thing, but Katie could tell something was off.

"Come in here anyway," Katie said. "You can tell me how things are going in the big city."

Sophie shuffled in and kissed her sister. "Isn't she cute?" she asked. "Michelle makes these visits worth it all."

Katie blinked. Since she was a business type, not a mental health practitioner like her sister, she went right to the point. "What do you mean, 'worth it all'? Don't you like seeing your dad and Kristen?"

"Yeah, they're okay. I've got a life, too, you know?"

Being careful to sound nonchalant, Katie answered, "Sure you do. I just meant they love to see you when you come. And Michelle is your baby sister, so you have to bond with her, right?"

Sophie flipped her long dark hair away from her face. "Yeah, I get to bond with every little kid around. My brother is in his 'terrible threes,' which is another bit of fun for me."

Katie remembered Sophie's mother had a child with her second husband. That made Sophie a half-sister twice over. She was no therapist, but it made sense that Sophie might not feel she fit in anywhere.

Munching her cheesy, meaty piece of pie, Katie served a small slice to Sophie on a paper plate. "That sounds hard. You're older than the other kids in your parents' houses, and there are different folks to deal with at each place."

To her relief, Sophie took the pizza and had a bite. "You bet," she mumbled with her mouth full. "Just when I get used to Kristen and Dad, I have to leave. Plus, all my friends have plans during our school breaks. But not me, never. My plans are always to come to itty-bitty Gordon."

"Also hard," Katie said, her own mouth stuffed with greasy deliciousness. "Have you talked to your mom and dad about this stuff?"

Sophie hooted. "Of course. NOT. My dad's so happy to see me I can't disappoint him. And your *sister* is almost as busy as Dad. We were supposed to have a girls' night when Michelle went to bed, but she forgot her important meeting. Here I sit, with *you*."

Katie squelched her temper. Sophie's tirade was meant to irritate. No sense in biting on the kid's bait. "That's tough, Soph. I'll bet Kristen makes it up to you. Girls' night may still happen when she gets back."

"We'll see," Sophie said as she walked back to the family room. "Good luck getting Michelle to bed without Kristen. See you later."

That was fun, Katie thought. Now she knew what Kristen meant about Sophie being a surprise. The charming little girl from Kristen's courtship and wedding to Mike had disappeared. This kid was a handful. And a little mean. Katie rethought her dreams of having a family and tended to Michelle, who continued to be happy enjoying her pizza crust bits. Maybe she should just get a goldfish or something.

Michelle went down with no fuss as Kristen promised. Katie grabbed a soft drink from the kitchen and joined Sophie, who was changing television channels faster than Katie could register.

"Hold it. You're going so fast. How do you know if the show is something you'd like?"

Sophie tossed the remote to Katie and shrugged. "There's nothing to like here. I'm going to bed." Sophie seemed to rethink her rudeness, and added, "It was good to see you, Katie. I'm glad you and your mom came back to Indiana."

And that's as good as she was going to get. The fish was looking better and better.

Kristen breezed in a few minutes later. "Where is everybody?" she asked.

"Because I always follow instructions, baby Michelle is tucked in and fast asleep." Katie winced and continued. "Sophie went to bed, too."

"We were supposed to have a girls' night," Kristen moaned. "Did she forget?"

"She remembered," Katie said. "I think she doubted it would happen."

"Cross my heart, I told her I'd be back by nine, in plenty of time for the movie she wanted to watch." Kristen looked forlorn, then angry. "Wait a sec. Did she imply that *I* forgot? That we weren't going to have our night together?"

Katie didn't want to get in the middle of this drama, one that looked like it was repeated often. "Ask her. She just went to her room a few minutes ago." She hugged her sister and put on her jacket. "I've got to head home. Have a good evening."

Snuggled in her bed with her favorite Jane Austin novel, Katie thought about recent events. Her move back to Indiana had been made in the throes of several mini crises. She and Dan were a disappointment as a couple, which they were both wise enough to know. Her mother had grieved her husband's death sufficiently to realize Gordon was where she belonged. And Katie's insurance job in Phoenix was a dead end if ever there was one. The irony was the change in Katie's view of her sister's life. Since Kristen's wedding to Mike, Katie had been sure the elder Anderson sister was living in heaven on earth. Great husband, ready-made family with a sweet baby added on, and tenure at GCC. Katie had envied Kristen from afar for quite a while now.

God was trying to teach her something. Perfection was not for this world, obviously. Sunday school had drilled that into her theological thinking way back. But it was so tempting to think there was a key, a trick, to make this life resemble the ideal promised by God. That was God's lesson, she figured. Faith and perseverance would get us far, but God remained at the center of our needs. Even the perfect Kristen Anderson had struggles. Katie sent up a quick prayer and snuggled deeper under the covers, thanking God for her blessings and vowing to help her sister more than she had in the past.

Work continued to flow well. She ran into Kristen at the GCC cafeteria a week after her stint with Michelle and Sophie. Her sister reported the rest of Sophie's visit had gone better, and that they did indeed have their girls' night after Katie left. Katie reminded her that she could help out whenever Kristen needed it; to her shock, her sister became tearful and hugged her after the offer was made.

Her office phone rang, interrupting her thoughts. Dean King's extension showed on the caller ID. Katie crossed her fingers. Figuring out her new boss was a challenge. He was smart, tough, fair, and always after the next big thing. Quite a combination for a woman new to the academic atmosphere.

"I've read your most recent report, Katie," the dean said. "Very impressive. You've gotten commitments from faculty members in several departments, with the exception of culinary arts. What's going on there?"

What's going on is nothing, Katie thought. She'd left several messages for the CA director, Louis Masson, and received no replies. Zero.

She decided to be honest. Dr. King didn't respond well to hedging. "I've tried to contact Professor Masson several times, with no success. Do you have any suggestions? I'd really like to include his students in the internship program. Restaurants are businesses, after all."

She could almost hear Dr. King's grin over the phone. He chuckled and said, "That they are, Katie. But that's exactly the wrong approach to take with Louis Masson. There are times when I think he should be in the *fine* arts department instead of *culinary* arts."

"You've lost me, Dr. King. What are you saying?"

"I'm saying you'll have to finesse Louis a little. Educate him about the need for his students to know the business side of the restaurant arena. But also talk to him about his background. You know about his history, correct?"

Nope, she didn't know anything about his history. The other faculty members hadn't required such research; in fact, they'd been happy to have help placing their students in ready-to-go internship slots.

"I'll be honest, Dr. King. I'll need to research Louis Masson and get back to you. Any suggestions about where to start?"

Dr. King chuckled again, this time longer and with more enjoyment. "Just your standard Google search, Katie. That's all you'll need to get the scoop on Louis Masson."

Okay, she could follow directions. Google was her friend. Katie tapped Louis Masson's name into the search engine and was astounded at the pages of linked information appearing instantly on her screen.

First, she read about Louis' training and employment history. He was a graduate of not one, but two culinary arts schools, both top-tier. At first glance, his spotty resume looked suspect, but a side search informed her that successful chefs often worked at several restaurants in sequence as they honed their skills. It wasn't at all unusual to move from place to place, often before finally opening an eponymous place of their own. Oddly, Louis had no self-titled restaurants to his credit.

What he did have in his online records were numerous photos of him with celebrities, European royals, and politicians. And not just images of him in his chef's garb, but in tuxedos at palaces and in casual attire on yachts, hobnobbing with the rich and famous. How in the name of all that was holy had he ended up at GCC?

Katie continued to study the pictures, which loaded one after the other as quickly as she could view them. Louis was a stunner, in a bad-boy kind of way. Dark, unkempt hair, permanent stubble, and flashing emerald eyes. He fit right in with all the beautiful people.

Those eyes. They could disarm anyone, with absolutely no effort on Louis' part. Katie found herself looking more closely. There was a combined challenge and sadness in those eyes. This man had something to prove. Maybe not a secret, but a hidden part of himself kept from others.

It was interesting that Louis was never photographed alone with a woman. Most of the women in the pictures looked at him with big smiles and occasionally adoration, but he was noncommittal, even in the candid shots. Those glamorous creatures were simply accessories to his leading-man persona. Ever the businesswoman, Katie wondered about his lack of attachment. Surely, he could have fallen for a wealthy heiress, one who could finance his restaurant dream. She knew she was being cynical and dark, but really.

Shaking herself, Katie regrouped. He was a fine-looking man, but also one who was short-changing his students by keeping them away from her program. Her task was to help him realize all his students could gain via her internships. So, how did a corn-fed woman from Indiana (with a little life experience in Arizona) engage a worldly man like Louis? Was that even possible?

Well, she'd done hard things before. She thought about searching for ways to charm a resistant man, but then caught herself. What had Louis been doing prior to coming to Gordon? His search data ended last year, with a photo at a British polo field. Maybe he'd gotten into trouble with drugs or alcohol. Or perhaps he was a good son who wanted to be closer to his mom and dad.

She doubted it was that simple. Something had instigated his move back to the U.S. Broken heart, perhaps. Whatever. She had some info, now her job was to convince Louis to participate in her internship program. Focusing on their commonalities, she decided to leave yet another message on his GCC extension, asking if he would like to join her for a dinner meeting.

After scripting and rehearsing, Katie spoke into Louis' voice mail. "Hi, Chef Masson. It's Katie Anderson again, calling about internships for your students. I wondered if you'd be free to meet for dinner some evening this week or next. There's a new farm-to-table restaurant about thirty minutes from Gordon that's supposed to highlight Indiana specialties. Fresh corn, berries, free-range chicken. The whole works. Do you have any openings this week or next?"

Surprised at her anxiety, Katie hung up and wiped her clammy hands on her pants. Dr. King had made it clear that Louis and his students had to participate in her program. It was hard to believe that one person could make or break her new career at GCC, but there it was. Louis Masson was the key to her success. She was both intrigued and angry.

Knowing she could do nothing but wait Louis out, Katie focused on tasks at hand. She was teaching an introductory level career exploration course and spent the next two hours grading her students' latest assignments. Ah, to be nineteen again and full of confidence! Each paper was more grandiose than the last—brain surgeon, superintendent of schools, business mogul. No one seemed to start their career small. She admitted there was nothing wrong with big goals. The second part of the assignment would be telling. The task was to research what education, training, and experience would be required for the student's stated goal. Hopefully, there would be more realism as she read on.

No, not much. The kid who wanted to be a brain surgeon simply said that "after years of schooling," he'd be doing surgeries at his pick of hospitals, with the goal of a job at an oceanside location. The school superintendent ignored the need for graduate school training and years of classroom experience, simply pointing out that as a recent public-school grad, she knew what the system needed.

Katie forced herself to read all twenty of the assignments. Most were fair, a few were realistic and optimistic, and the bottom few were those she'd read first. There was relief in that. She'd have to ask her sister the psychologist how to motivate young people to set goals more in line with their talents and willingness to work. But she knew, psychologist or not, that Kristen would say there was no magic solution.

Also of concern were the responses that glossed over the difficulties of raising a family while working at a prestigious dream job. Katie was single with no children, but she saw plenty of angst in Kristen as she juggled baby Michelle's needs while giving her job her best effort. Mike, Kristen's husband, was a good dad and had to balance both his job and his children, one of whom was a tween going through a tough patch. Katie shuddered as she remembered Sophie's behavior a few Fridays ago. Sophie was a good kid, but she gave Kristen and Mike a run for their money.

Guest speakers were slated to come weekly to the career exploration class. Katie hoped against hope that hearing from someone other than her would influence her class members. Surely having a practicing surgeon (general, not brain) speak about her career and family challenges would convince folks that lofty goals were worthy, as long as there was commitment to work and time to achieve them.

Katie was startled into the present at the sound of the laughing students in the hallway outside her door. Her mental admonitions to her students sounded just like her father had when he'd lectured her about wanting to get her MBA. She had been bored at her job and convinced that a shiny new degree would solve all her problems. Dad had pointed out the grueling two-year schedule at the grad program she'd been admitted to, including long weekends out of town each month, online meetings with her cohort every Friday night until after ten, and reams of papers and case studies to read and analyze. All this while working full-time, he'd said. Plus, she would have no life for over two years and would deplete her meager savings.

Digging in, Katie had argued but persisted in her goal. Dad had been right. The program was tough, the hours exhausting, and the group projects a joke at times. Inevitably, "group" was code for one or two people doing all the work. But now Katie had her MBA from a stellar program, and it had all been worth it. Gordon Community College had been happy to hire her and she bid her insurance job a not-so-fond farewell.

She thought back to her nineteen-year-old self. What would have persuaded her to set realistic goals? Or was the point to mature a little and then realize what your goals really were? Was it really fair to expect young people to predict what their interests would be in ten or twenty years? Maybe career planning should be more fluid. Yeah, parents would love that. They were paying tuition for their kids to be self-sufficient, not to float from one job to another.

Katie sighed. It was five-thirty and Louis Masson had ignored her plea again. Time to go home and microwave a frozen dinner. Turkey with dressing sounded good and would be ready in minutes instead of hours. Yum.

There was a brief knock at her door followed by the presence of an unmistakable male. He was wearing the standard faculty outfit of khakis, long-sleeved shirt with the sleeves rolled up, and trendy athletic shoes. Louis Masson had deigned to make an appearance.

Chapter Three

"Did I just hear you mutter something about a fat-headed fake gourmet?" Louis asked. "Surely there can't be two of me on this campus."

Katie stared at the man who had casually planted himself in the side chair at her desk. Had she said that out loud? Time to regroup.

"Just muttering to myself after a long day," she said. "How nice to finally meet you, Chef Masson."

"Louis is fine," he answered smoothly. "May I call you Katie?"

Noting he pronounced his name, "Louie," Katie's opinion of the fatheaded guy was reinforced. "Of course. To what do I owe the pleasure of this in-person visit?"

"I'd say the visit has been prompted by your twelve voice mail messages over the course of the last two weeks," Louis said. "I guessed it was time for me to respond."

It sure was, Katie thought. *Past time. And it wasn't twelve messages, you twit. Six at the most.* She paused and waited for Louis to continue.

Looking surprised at her silence, Louis said, "I've been very busy with the semester. But that doesn't excuse my lack of communication. I'll admit I was intrigued by your invitation to a dinner meeting at the restaurant you mentioned. I've been to that place. They do a serviceable job, given their lack of training and the limited ingredients they have to work with."

Fine. Now his cards were on the table. Snob, through and through. "Well, I wouldn't want to have our initial meeting at a place beneath your standards. Where would you suggest?" Katie deliberately made the dinner meeting a sure thing. Louis wasn't going to weasel out of talking to her.

"I think the essence of fine dining is being true to what a restaurant does best. The best I've found within an hour's drive is the cafeteria in Mooresville. Would that be acceptable to you, Katie?"

Katie's eyes sparkled. She loved that place. They served huge portions, so she got at least three meals out of each visit. The starches (mashed potatoes, mac and cheese, stuffing, noodles…) were to die for. Katie was a spirit animal for a good Midwestern cafeteria.

"That would be perfect," she said. "Hearty food and no waitstaff to bother us as we discuss how our programs can help each other."

Louis' brow pinched. "Quality waitstaff are an integral part of the dining experience," he said with a patronizing eye roll. "But you're right, not at a cafeteria." He paused and seemed to reflect on his next words. "To be honest, I'm unsure how our programs can actually help each other."

Katie's eyes widened. Again, she waited Louis out.

Forced to keep talking, he looked at the ceiling and exhaled the next rush of words. "My program can help yours by providing students so that your internship slots will be filled. Dr. King will love that. But your internships can only harm my program, obviously."

"Beg your pardon?"

"Really, Katie, it's perfectly clear. You have no food service or gourmet cooking experience. Your focus is solely on the business aspects of restaurants. My students will end up interning at fast food, or at best, sit-down places whose 'chefs' microwave frozen products ordered by the corporate office. High fat, high-sodium foods with the best profit margins are the entrees of choice. I have enough trouble convincing my students to prepare healthy, innovative dishes. I won't have them contaminated by one of your subpar restaurant placements."

Katie managed to look interested, even partly convinced. She was instead contemplating how she would attack Louis Masson if given the chance. She could plant an article in the campus newspaper stating that he relied on frozen dinners when no one was looking. Or maybe she would just maim him, smash his chopping hand with an iron skillet. That had appeal. Anyone this condescending and superior didn't deserve to make food for others. She was not a violent person, but good grief.

Instead, she smiled. Her mother called it her lethal smile, the one with lots of dimples and teeth, but with no sparkle in her eyes. Time to work on Louis.

"I see I've got lots to learn, Louis. I'm so glad we're going to talk about all this over dinner. Grab your phone, open up your calendar, and let's set this meeting up. How is next Tuesday evening for you?"

Louis looked disappointed at Katie's agreeable response. He was baiting her, she knew, but he wasn't that good at it. When it came to a good give-and-take with obstinate men, those European celebs must be amateurs compared to Indiana-bred women.

After some back-and-forth, they settled on Thursday evening for their dinner. Louis had a food lab on Tuesday evenings, something about sauces and stocks, which Katie knew could be bought at any basic grocery store. Cooking them from scratch seemed a bit much to her. Then she had another inspiration.

"I've got it! Louis, we can meet for our meal on Thursday, but I can also attend your Tuesday lab. What better way for me to get a sense of your culinary devotion than to see the master at work?"

Louis grinned. "Now I understand, Katie. I'm the master, huh? See you Tuesday at four. I'll expect you to bring your own hairnet. My department will supply a lab coat."

Walking to his car, Louis reflected on his impressions of Katie Anderson. He knew she was the sister of Kristen Sutliff, a psych professor. He liked Kristen. She had been assigned as his faculty mentor and was helpful in teaching him now to navigate the sometimes choppy waters of academia. He'd learned a lot in a short time—basically, that his experience, culinary awards, and European contacts meant nothing at GCC.

Katie was not only different from her sister in personality, but also in appearance. While Kristen was tall, athletic-looking, and sported butterscotch ringlets, her younger sister seemed like a foundling in comparison. Katie was petite, with straight dark hair that tended to fall over one eye while she spoke. Probably this was caused by her habit of talking with her hands and her slightly dramatic air. She was also skilled in catching him off guard. Just when he thought she was going to engage in his insults, she paused and waited him out. So, she was a smart woman, to a degree.

Smart, but not in his arena. He doubted he would ever let his students work at one of her internship sites. Where could they go in this backward town that could possibly benefit their careers? Even Indianapolis had slim pickings when it came to quality restaurants that weren't chains run by corporate moguls. There was no way Katie Anderson had the contacts or expertise to land those placements.

He wasn't being facetious when he voiced his concerns about contaminating his chefs in training. Once out of his two-year program, they would have their pick of culinary schools, and in those places, they would hone their skills. *Not* in some Indiana greasy spoon.

He missed Europe. It had life, stimulation, and enough drama to keep him entertained. Of course, it also had women who viewed him as a more delicious feast than his food. His memories of the women were plentiful but shallow. After a time, the casual encounters left him oddly dissatisfied. And then last year, his mother called.

Nothing was really wrong, she'd insisted. His father just needed rest and appropriate treatment. And she'd been correct. His father responded well to the chemo and was doing fine. Nonetheless, he was happy he'd returned to the U.S. and to his parents.

It was time to build a life in his own country.

Too bad that life had to be at GCC. Teaching was Louis' new passion, but he was surprised at the lack of faculty posts available on short notice. GCC wanted him to build their new culinary program and he was glad to oblige. But Gordon, Indiana, was a sinkhole. If you hadn't been born here, didn't know how everyone was related by blood or marriage or divorce, and couldn't grasp the appeal of high school basketball, you were out of luck. *He* was out of luck.

But not totally. He enjoyed his weekends in Indianapolis. He would visit his parents, cook dinner for them, and catch up on their plans. Currently they were saving for two months of winter in Florida, a cliché even Louis could tolerate. Indiana winters had never been his favorite. Cold weather without the benefit of mountains or glacial scenery was a waste of God's effort in his opinion.

After spending time with his parents, Louis would explore Indy, the city of his birth and early years. By the time he reached high school age, he'd earned a stint at Culver Academy in northern Indiana. After he'd "borrowed" a friend's car, the years at Culver had shifted his focus for the better. Oddly enough, he actually had a GCC contact of sorts through his years at Culver. Annie Upton's husband, Ben, had been a classmate of his, sent by his own unnerved parents when they couldn't control his adolescent behavior. So, there it was, Louis was actually a member of Gordon's elite. He had a connection with a fellow GCC employee not involving their shared place of work.

Louis spent the evening planning his weekend. After time with his mom and dad, he'd go to the art museum and then purchase the items needed for Tuesday's lab. Students needed to know how to make a quality stock, and bones from the meat section at Gordon's big-box grocery wouldn't be good enough. He knew he was being elitist, but the meat market in downtown Indy would provide the best carcasses around. These were the only times he missed being a chef; having access to the best ingredients was crucial.

His attention to detail would be lost on Katie Anderson. She would wonder what the fuss was about. Chances were her closest experience with stock came in a red and white can.

Katie focused on her weekend chores and enjoyed planning the menu for dinner with her mother. Kristen and Mike begged off, since Sophie was back at her mother's home in Indianapolis. They had a sitter for Michelle and planned a date night for themselves.

Kaye arrived with the obligatory bottle of wine, as always forgetting that Katie liked aged bourbon. Despite her lapse, Kaye did enthuse over the smells coming from the kitchen.

"It's that 'engagement chicken' recipe that the internet's been raving about," Katie explained. "It's roast chicken with veggies and garlic. Even I can handle it, and with a couple of convenient sides, it's a good meal."

"*Of course,* you can handle it," Kaye said. "You're quite a good cook, Katie. Why would you doubt that?"

Her mother's instincts were as sharp as ever. Katie

decided to be open about the situation with Louis. "It's the culinary arts prof at GCC," she said. "I've got to win him over to let his students participate in my program. Dr. King implied it's a given, almost a mandate. But the great Louis Masson doesn't think his trainees will benefit from internships."

"It's more than that," Kaye said. "What else?"

"Good point, Mom," Katie said, wincing as she took a sip of the slightly bitter wine. "Chef Masson is just too superior, too sophisticated, too worldly. I can't believe he's at GCC. I know the administration views his presence as a coup, but why would he come here?"

"Maybe for the same reasons we came back," Kaye said. "Could be family ties, wanting to be closer to home, all that. And maybe his pretensions hide an insecurity. Who knows?"

Kaye took a much more robust swallow of her wine than Katie and continued. "Other than his abrasive personality, what's he like?"

"He's driven to give his students a quality experience," Katie admitted. "Based on my internet research, he's won awards and is at the top of his field." Katie grinned, knowing her mother would love the next part. "And the photos are quite revealing. He was friends with lots of the rich and famous of Europe and the Middle East. He must think Gordon is the pits."

Kaye relished those tidbits, as Katie knew she would. "And he's a looker, right? Handsome in a bad-boy way? Bedroom eyes?"

"Mom! What's gotten into you?"

"I'm old, but I'm still breathing, honey. You gave me your answer. This Louis fellow has you off balance in a lot of ways." Both women laughed, enjoying their camaraderie.

The engagement chicken lived up to its reputation, and later they enjoyed a pumpkin cake for dessert. Kaye continued to challenge Katie's insecurities in the kitchen.

"Honey, this cake is wonderful. Was it difficult to make?"

"No, the box mix was very specific with its instructions," Katie teased. "I just added oil, egg, and water. The glaze only required water. My kind of baking."

"Never mind," Kaye said. "I want you to promise me this Louis person won't get you down. And the idea of one person derailing your career at GCC is ridiculous. No one should have that much power."

Let her be right, dear Lord, Katie prayed. After her mother's exit and a quick kitchen cleanup, Katie settled in to read her novel. Her mother was correct. If Louis Masson had enough power to ruin her, GCC wasn't a healthy place to work. There were lots of jobs in Indy. She had options.

Despite her positive self-talk and another coaching session from her mother, by Tuesday afternoon Katie was a jumble of nerves. She also looked foolish in her hairnet, which jammed her thick dark locks into a helmet of hair. Weren't there other options for sanitary cooking? She'd seen shower cap type things on television, and they were a lot more flattering than the hairnet Louis had mandated. As she entered the food lab, Louis caught her eye and grinned. He was already laughing at her. Determined, Katie smiled back and walked up to him.

"I'm ready and dressed as you ordered," she said with a mock salute. "What's next?"

"You're here mostly to observe, Katie. My students are preparing three different recipes for beef stock. One is the traditional French method, and the other two require less time. The last one takes only an hour. I started the longer batches last night so the lab would be complete today." Louis looked at her carefully and added, "Even the most unsophisticated palates can tell the difference. We'll see how you do in the blind taste test."

That was enough for Katie. She briefly thought about playing the stuffy-nose allergy card but decided to honor Louis' rules and give her honest opinion on each product. If she failed the taste challenge, so be it.

But Louis wasn't finished taunting her. "I assume you know the difference between stock and broth," he said. "Right?"

"Let me think," Katie said with mock seriousness, pointer finger on her chin. "I believe stock has more gelatin due to the presence of the bones in which it was cooked. Broth is made with meat, not bones."

"How did you know that?" Louis asked, looking surprised. He knitted his brows. Katie enjoyed his irritation.

"Doesn't everyone know the difference?" she asked.

"No, they don't," Louis said. "Have you had culinary training? Or high school home ec?"

Katie wished she had formal training and was about to inform Louis that most high schools had eliminated home economics courses long ago. To the students' detriment, in her opinion.

"No formal training," she answered. "And my high school didn't offer home ec."

Maybe a Girl Scout badge? Louis wondered.

Katie gave in. "Food Network," she announced. "I've learned a lot from watching television. Sorry, Louis. Maybe your knowledge base isn't as special as you think."

Louis smiled. "Maybe not. In all fairness, that channel provides some good education about food selection and techniques." He continued to smile as he kept careful watch on his students' work. "But it also showcases silly competitions and terrible knife skills. You have to be selective about what you think you're learning."

"Whatever," Katie said, matching his smile. "When do I get to taste the different batches of stock?"

Louis directed his students to set up the blind tasting stations. "Right now," he said. "We will all sample the stocks and record our impressions on the tasting cards. No talking allowed."

The tasting commenced, results were disclosed, and Katie landed in the middle of the pack in terms of accuracy. She incorrectly rated the quickest stock over the middle one but was accurate about the long-cooking stock having the most depth of flavor. Louis, of course, didn't participate since he knew which stocks were which.

By six o'clock the lab was cleaned, and the students headed out for their evenings. Katie freed herself from the awful hairnet, finger-combed her hair, and followed them out. Louis stopped her as she entered the parking lot.

"Where to now, Katie? Want to get coffee?" Louis looked relaxed and confident.

"I'm on my way home," she said. "Coffee isn't good for me this late in the day. And I have papers to grade before tomorrow."

"Papers? You're teaching?"

"I teach a career exploration course. It draws students who are uncertain about their majors, and those who are interested in a lot of things and don't have a clue about their future plans. Sometimes I think Kristen should be teaching it, not me. Often, we enter into tough psychological areas, like parental expectations, self-doubt, and working for money versus passion."

Louis studied Katie. He nodded and said, "Those are tough areas. I would know about the money versus passion thing. If you ever need a guest speaker, let me know."

Katie stared at the man who had spent most of the last two weeks demeaning her and her job. Now he was offering to help her. What had changed?

"You're on," she said softly. "We can compare calendars at dinner on Thursday and set something up."

Thursday came much too quickly for Katie. Louis had been human, almost nice at the end of Tuesday's lab. She preferred the snotty Louis. She was adept at dealing with men who thought they were superior. Nice guy Louis was an unknown quantity. What would he be like at dinner tonight?

They met at the cafeteria in Mooresville by mutual agreement. Their schedules were such that driving together would have been cumbersome. Katie was grateful for the small win.

"You go first," Katie ordered. "Dinner is my treat, so I'll pay for our two trays. Eat up!"

Louis chose his dinner carefully. Spinach salad with vinaigrette, lightly seared cod, Brussels sprouts, and a whole wheat roll rounded out his choices. He passed on dessert. Since Katie planned to get more than one meal from this outing, she was just as careful, but less refined. Let him think what he liked. She was going to eat with gusto.

Katie paid and followed Louis to their table. They emptied their trays and arranged their food. Louis was looking at Katie's choices, eyebrows raised, and lips pursed. "What?" she asked.

"Look at your food," he growled. "Chicken tenders, macaroni and cheese, mashed potatoes with wallpaper-paste gravy, and coconut cream pie. You eat like a seven-year-old."

Katie smiled, thanking God that Louis was back to his old self. She could deal with his ridicule much more easily than his sweetness. "You make a point," she said. "I love comfort foods, and the portions here will feed me for a while. To each his or her own, right?"

"Perhaps," Louis said, after a mincing bite of his salad. "Health should factor in as well, however. Do you have any idea of the fat grams on your side of the table?"

"There are lots, I know," Katie answered with another of her killer smiles. "Which would be a problem if I ate like this all the time. I don't. Balance is more important than avoiding pleasure, don't you think?"

Louis arched his brow. Katie continued before he could hit back. "If your students don't learn about balance, about the craft of combining artfully created food with a healthy financial picture, they'll be cooking for themselves alone. No restaurant, no matter how many stars it has in its Michelin rating, can exist for long without making money."

Louis frowned and stood, got a to-go box from the station a few feet away, and put the remainder of his dinner in it. "See you, Katie. I'm not hungry anymore."

Katie watched him leave and could see him get in his car. She'd blown it. Their evening was over. She hadn't even scheduled him to talk to her career exploration class. What a pretentious snob. How did a man manage to be so sure, so confident, so entitled? And how in the world was she going to convince him she could educate his students?

Chapter Four

Louis drove to his home outside Gordon, using his phone GPS to navigate the unfamiliar path from Mooresville. Why had he let Katie Anderson get to him? She had stated the obvious. Restaurants were businesses, dependent on a healthy cash flow if they were to survive. Where they differed was in the area of what was best for his students. If young chefs in training were exposed to the realities of chain eateries, and to their generous (compared to those of gourmet kitchens) starting salaries, none of his graduates would go on to make their mark in the culinary world.

Not that it mattered in the big picture. He'd made his mark, and when the time came for him to branch out to establish his own restaurant, he'd come home instead. Dad had been sick, true. But Louis had lacked the crucial element of a successful artist—a ready supply of cash or the willingness (or subservience) to be financed by someone with an agenda. The duchess's agenda was simple. She wanted Louis to marry her, father some kids, and look good in the society pages. His other option for investment funds, a Saudi prince, had insisted on non-negotiable veto power over the menu. No restaurant was worth those concessions.

If he were honest with himself, he had been more than ready to return to the U.S. Restaurant hours, especially when combined with appearances at parties covered by all the glossy magazines, were exhausting. He wasn't that young anymore. At thirty-five, he wanted a life beyond working until two in the morning, sleeping until three in the afternoon, and starting it all again. He thanked God, again, for the wisdom of avoiding the drug scene. The stimulants offered in nearly every restaurant setting were standard fare. Louis believed in healthy living, even when he was putting in workaholic hours.

So, why did the opinion of a woman who would barely qualify as a kitchen porter matter at all? Sure, Katie knew her way around stocks and broths, but her education about quality food probably ended at bagged salads and sheet pan dinners.

There had to be a middle ground. Dr. King was intent on Louis' students participating in Katie's program. He imagined Katie was under similar pressure from Dr. King. Despite their differences, it looked like he and Katie would have to work together.

Unless he continued to act like a spoiled brat as he just had at the cafeteria. Katie was like a dog with a bone when it came to her career and internship program, but what had he expected? Had he wanted their dinner to be more like a social event? Or, God forbid, like a date?

He laughed at the thought as he entered the exit

ramp for Gordon. Katie's looks would never make it in the brittle social scene of Europe. She was pretty, beautiful in fact, but not up to the standards of expert makeup artists. Her looks were completely natural and would be ruined by exotic sculpting and highlighting techniques. He liked the way she presented herself to the world, comfortable with herself. He especially enjoyed her big chocolate-brown eyes. They missed nothing and let him get away with nothing. Perhaps that's what had felt off with the duchess. Her eyes followed his, always mirroring what he was feeling and ready to be in total agreement with whatever he said or felt. It was stifling in its way, always being told you were right, that you could do no wrong. It actually became boring.

He had to make this evening right. Pulling into the deserted bank parking lot in Gordon, he entered Katie's cell number into his phone. She picked up after only one ring.

"What now, Louis?" she asked. "What else did I do to ruin your evening? Are you feeling nauseous? Stomach cramping? I'd be glad to make a pharmacy run. I owe you, after all."

Her sarcasm made him smile again. This woman was not boring, not at all. "No, I'm fine. I'm calling to apologize. There was no excuse for my behavior tonight. Let's push the reset button if we can. How about dinner this weekend? I'll cook for you."

Silence greeted his mea culpa. Katie had either crashed her car or was refusing to answer. Louis was worried. Either option wasn't good.

"Um, okay," Katie said. "You don't have to cook, though. There's a good restaurant twenty minutes from Gordon. It's not up to your standards, but the

Indianapolis city magazine praised its innovative take on standard diner dishes."

"Cooking is the best way I know to set things right between us," Louis said. "I'm sincere, Katie. I'm really sorry."

Sensing her unwillingness, Louis forced himself to sell her on dinner at his place. "You can even pick the menu, Katie. I'll fry some chicken and make a cheese pizza if you want."

"Okay," Katie mumbled. "See you on Saturday at six. Text me your address."

With that, the call was over. Louis decided to believe he'd saved the evening. He knew he was wrong, but then again, Katie was coming for dinner in two days. He'd salvaged a bit of their relationship. Professional relationship.

The second she ended the puzzling call with Louis, Katie called her mother. Kaye would have some insight. Her mom's old-fashioned radar was usually more than accurate.

"You're saying he had a tantrum, walked out, and then called to apologize?" Kaye asked. "Did he think you'd flirt with him? It was a business dinner, right?"

"That's my point, Mom," Katie said. "Do you think he wanted it to be more social? That I offended him by bringing up the internship issue instead of trying to get to know him better? That can't be it."

"We can't really know, honey. But the important thing is that he tried to make amends, though I don't like his offer to fry chicken and make you a cheese pizza. How condescending."

"He says I eat like a little kid," Katie groaned.

"And I guess I do, sometimes."

Kaye was having none of it. "You eat like an Indiana woman, though most of us could do with fewer calories," she said. "Louis Masson has a lot to learn, not only about his home state, but about proper manners. His stint in Europe with the rich and infamous has trained him to be rude. He'll sort things out, I'm sure of it. Or GCC will humble him. Or both."

Katie thanked her mother and they made plans to meet on Sunday to discuss the Saturday meal with Louis. She also thanked God for her loving family. She sensed Louis didn't have the support she did from those he loved.

Kaye moved to her front porch swing to watch the sunset. Katie's call had upset her, but she didn't know why. Katie was a smart woman, and she would handle Louis with success. As she sighed, a voice called from the sidewalk.

"Are you all right, Kaye? Anything wrong?"

Ah, the resident hunk. Too bad Linda wasn't with her. She'd love to talk to Bob about all her concerns. Kaye, on the other hand, wanted to be alone.

"I'm fine, Bob. I've discovered you never stop worrying about your kids. But my girls are bright and accomplished, so I'm making too much of minor things." Kaye paused and forced herself to be cordial. After all, she didn't want to be in the same category as Louis Masson.

"How are you, Bob? Anything new?" Before she knew it, he was next to her on the swing. Being polite backfired.

"Nothing big," he replied. "Although I understand your dilemma completely. My kids are doing well, but I live with all their challenges as if they were my own. I trust them, know they're more than capable, but I want their lives to be perfect. There's no such thing on this earth, is there?"

Kaye looked at him, trying to focus in the dusky light. He was saying the right things, and his words comforted her. But he was still Bob Benson, and he'd hurt Kristen. In the spirit of Kristen's forgiveness, she decided to let her anger go for the moment.

"No, not on this earth," she replied. "Thanks for understanding, Bob. Maybe we love our kids too much. Or we're just stuck in the phase of life where we're pretty content and want our children to have that same peace."

Shifting toward her, Bob leaned in. "Are you content, Kaye? Is living here alone enough for you?" Catching himself, he sat back. "I'm not saying it well, I know. But there are times when I'd like to share more of my life with someone else. I'm at peace with my life, not anxious about a job or finances, fairly healthy, but I guess I'm lonely. Do you ever feel that way?"

Kaye wasn't sure if this was a generic discussion about aging or Bob's way of getting closer to her. She decided to take the generic road. "Well, Kristen says people were meant to be connected with others. Lots of research bears it out, she says. That's why I like living here. There are lots of folks around to enjoy life with."

"You know that's not what I meant," Bob said, looking away at the streetlamp. "I was talking about having one special person in your life."

Well, they weren't on the generic road anymore. Kaye decided to go with Bob's actual meaning. "I do miss Stan," she said. "Sometimes so much it hurts physically. But the thought of having that type of love again seems impossible."

"Agreed," Bob said. "We'll never have what we had before. But could there be another type of love for us oldsters?"

Kaye laughed, grateful Bob had lightened the mood. "Oldsters! There's a new label for us! Better than seniors. When I hear that one, I think I'm ready to graduate high school again."

Bob laughed and stood to leave. "It was good to talk, Kaye. Hang in there with your daughters. As you said, they're smart women. They'll be fine."

He paused on the top step of the porch. "It's not Kristen, is it? I'd hate to think she's still dealing with the aftereffects of my prideful behavior a few years ago."

Kaye shook her head. "No, Kristen is fine. She's a mom to a baby and stepmom to a challenging girl, but her career is fine." Standing, she went to the porch railing, not too close to Bob, but close enough for a deeper conversation. "I know you're sorry for ruining Kristen's semester so long ago, but she's convinced me it was all for the best. She's better at forgiveness than I am. But I'm trying, Bob."

Bob's smile reflected the last rays of the setting sun. "I'm happy to hear that, Kaye. What about a meal out to celebrate our friendship? We could head to Indianapolis next weekend for dinner and the symphony."

This guy doesn't quit, Kaye reflected. She'd said she was *trying* to forgive, but he took it for granted.

"We can celebrate, but let's stick to Gordon," she answered. "How's that?"

"I'll take it," Bob said, still smiling as if he'd won the lottery. "We'll talk this week about the details when we walk."

Let's hope Linda isn't walking that day, Kaye thought. This little celebration could get tricky fast. She suddenly realized the negative aspects of living in a retirement community made small-town intrigue look like child's play.

But what of it? Linda would understand. Kaye was going out with Bob as a mark of their newly established peace. Linda knew the story of Bob's unfair treatment of Kristen. She was a mother; she'd understand that Kaye was moving on but was still wary of Bob's character. Kaye's phone rang, and Linda's name appeared on the screen. Perfect.

"Hi, Linda. What's going on with you on this beautiful evening?" Kaye knew she was playing for time, but there it was. She was nervous.

"Was that Bob Benson on your porch?" Linda asked, or rather accused. "What were you two talking about? It looked very cozy."

"Not cozy, just a friendly chat about our kids and all that."

No fool, Linda wasn't buying Kaye's deflection. "I disagree, Kaye. It looked almost intimate from my vantage point. What's up?"

"What's up is that we're building our friendship, Linda. Bob hurt my daughter, as you know, and I've been late to the forgiveness table. I decided it was time to let it all go. Kristen has, after all. But more to the point, were you spying on me?"

Linda sputtered her reply. "Spying? Of course

not! But I happened to look down the street and saw you two practically on top of each other."

"Linda, that's ridiculous. We were standing upright! Tell me what's really bothering you." As if Kaye didn't know.

"I like Bob," Linda huffed. "You know that. I'd think you'd back off, just out of loyalty to our friendship."

"I am loyal to our friendship," Kaye said quietly. "But I'm also open to other friendships. It seems to me you should tell Bob about your feelings and see if he reciprocates."

Linda was silent for several seconds. Finally, she answered, "He doesn't reciprocate, and you know it, Kaye. It hurts. I feel like I'm in middle school. But I'll get over it." After another period of quiet, Linda continued, "Be careful, Kaye. Bob has a mean streak, and your daughter lived it. He's not to be trusted."

Kaye sighed into the phone. "Yes, trust is a tricky thing. That's why Bob and I are friends, not lovers or business partners. You take care, Linda."

Saturday arrived with Louis reflecting on his conversation with Dr. King yesterday. They had met as each walked to the parking lot after a long week. Dr. King's message had been clear. GCC was fortunate to have Katie Anderson on staff and Louis should make every effort to work with her.

Louis had thought *he* was the one GCC was fortunate to have on staff, but Dr. King made his point. Academia required a little more teamwork than the standard gourmet kitchen, though kitchens required plenty. Maybe GCC needed a different type of teamwork, with emphasis on the team instead of a chef dictating and supervising every move. Good thing he'd invited Katie for dinner.

He fried the chicken using plenty of buttermilk and panko breading, along with an herb mixture he'd developed in France. The pizza required more innovation. Louis finally settled on a four-cheese mixture topped with gorgonzola. In addition to the cheeses, the pie was topped with thinly sliced apples, adding just enough sweetness to offset the bitter flavors. He placed the odds at fifty-fifty whether Katie would like it.

His doorbell rang promptly at six. Louis smiled at Katie on his porch, decked out in her distinctive dressy, yet casual attire. Her black slacks were topped with a sleeveless printed top, covered by a cashmere cardigan. Her dark hair was swept to one side, with gentle waves falling over her shoulder. And she'd worn strappy heels, a definite change from her usual ballet flats at work. He liked the effect and realized he appreciated her effort.

Katie handed him a bottle of wine and said, "I wasn't sure what you liked, but this is from a winery outside of Bloomington. You can sample it for research purposes if nothing else."

"Thank you, Katie," he said. "You didn't have to bring anything. This is my forgiveness dinner, remember?"

"I remember," she said, with a half-smile. "I just hope I don't screw it up."

Their laughter carried them into the kitchen, with Katie giving his home the once-over. "I love your place," she said. "I wouldn't have guessed you'd live in a farmhouse halfway to Indy. And you've kept the historic vibe while updating what needed to be improved."

"Thanks again," Louis said, surprised at how much her praise meant to him. "This house reminded me of the houses in the English countryside. Obviously, it's much newer, but I liked the lack of pretension. It's a farmhouse, and proud to be one."

Katie stared. "That's exactly right," she said. "You've been true to its nature, if there is such a thing in decorating terminology." She sat at the kitchen island and sniffed. "I smell fried chicken, for sure, but something else as well. When I was little, we called it 'stinky cheese'."

Fine. She'd like the chicken, but the pizza was probably not going to be a success. "It's a gourmet pizza, Katie. I doubt it will be your favorite, but it was a bestseller at my last restaurant. It was known as a good choice when young people had been out on the town and needed something rich to soak up all the alcohol in their systems."

"In Indiana, we gravitate to fries or tacos for that same remedy," Katie said. "Cheap yet effective."

Trying to be diplomatic, Louis said, "I see." He uncorked the wine and offered Katie a glass. She sipped, studying him.

"Are you all right, Louis? You seem a little edgy."

He considered changing the subject but decided to be honest. "I'm a little nervous," he admitted. "Dr. King told me we need to work together. I hope I've not ruined any chance of that."

Katie grinned. "Since I've gotten the same message from Dr. King, you haven't ruined anything. We just need to figure out how to meet each other's needs and still be true to our moral philosophies."

Suddenly aware of the possible implication of her words, pink spread up her cheeks.

Louis loved it. "I'm all for meeting each other's needs," he teased. "Tell me more."

"Professional needs," Katie stammered. "I need to fill my restaurant internship slots and you need to refer students to me. That's all I meant."

"Of course," Louis said with a smirk. "Tell me about the internship slots. We have a few minutes before the food is ready."

Katie detailed the positions ready for culinary arts students. As Louis had suspected, they were all chain restaurants. His learners would receive absolutely no cooking experience. He didn't count time spent defrosting food in the microwave as anything near cooking.

Despite that, he knew he had to work with Katie. He tried to be diplomatic. "Have you talked with the managers about what my students would do? What would their duties be?"

Katie studied him with that squinty-eyed look of hers. "As you probably suspect, they would learn all aspects of a chain operation, from adequate scheduling to entree prep." She took another sip of wine and sighed. "Some of the entrees are not made on site, but some are. One of the restaurants has a very precise method of cooking steaks. Surely that would benefit your students, Louis. Even gourmet restaurants pride themselves on their steaks."

Before he could comment, Katie went on. She looked nervous, as if allowing him to talk would ruin the evening. Which it might, he had to admit.

"And budgeting, ordering, and managing the food on hand. Most of the chains offer daily specials, often consisting of food that needs to be used. The dishes can be very innovative, Louis."

When she finally paused, after draining her glass, Louis ushered her into the dining room. "All good points, Katie, but it's time to eat. Let me get things organized."

He refused her offer of help and fumed in the kitchen as he made the appetizer tray of pizza slices and Caprese salad on skewers. He knew she was glossing over the actual experiences his students would have in the restaurants she had on her internship list. His kids would be filling in for call-ins, maybe even working the host stand, learning almost nothing from the time spent away from his classes.

"Ah, the stinky cheese," Katie breathed, as he entered the dining room. "Are those apples on the pizza?"

"They are the perfect complement to the strongly-flavored cheeses," Louis said. As Katie took a bite he asked, "What do you think?"

What she thought was evident. She grimaced and took a gulp from the water glass at her place setting. "My palate isn't very sophisticated, as we've already discussed," she said. "The taste is quite interesting."

Louis knew educating Katie on the subtleties of the flavors was a lost cause. "That's okay, Katie. I appreciate you giving the pizza a try. Help yourself to the skewers and I'll be back with the chicken and sides."

The fried chicken, sour cream mashed potatoes, and fresh green beans were a hit, of course. Katie raved over the breading on her chicken leg, the tang of the potatoes, and the almonds in the green beans. In another life, Louis could imagine introducing

Katie to the wonders of all the culinary options available around the world, but he knew it was a dream. Katie liked what she liked, and that was it.

As they spooned their sorbet in the living room, Katie went back to business. "Thanks for the lovely meal, Louis. I'm sorry my taste buds aren't worthy of your pizza. But what about our discussion before dinner? Do you think you'd let your students work for my internship sites?"

"I'm not sure," Louis said. "I'm being honest, Katie. I just don't know."

"When I'm stumped, I always ask myself what I'm afraid of," Katie said. "What's your fear about sending your students to work a measly fifteen hours a week for one semester at a chain restaurant? What are you really afraid of, Louis?"

Now it was Louis' turn to level the squinty eye. "I'm afraid of nothing, Katie. And everything."

Chapter Five

Katie looked at Louis and wondered what his cryptic comment was about. Afraid of everything? She doubted it. This guy was too full of himself to be afraid. She, however, was afraid of a lot. Mostly about whether coming back to Indiana had been a good idea. At least her insurance job hadn't been dependent on the whim of a chef who liked moldy cheese.

She arched her brow and silently dared Louis to continue.

He cleared his throat and took her cue. "I'm not afraid of challenges, Katie. Usually, they've worked out well for me. But lately I'm more cautious. My dad's cancer brought things home for me, no pun intended. The world looks more uncertain, more tenuous. Things can go bad in an instant. Maybe I need your sister's help with all this."

Katie shook her head. "No, you're describing what I feel, too. I don't think we need a therapist. You love your dad and want him with you for a long time. My mom says I need more faith. She could be right, but church has never been my scene. Too much hypocrisy."

Louis smiled and reached for her hand. "Your mother sounds like mine. When dad was ill, she never wavered. She knew God would get them through." He squeezed her fingers and let go. "With regard to church, I used to be similar to you. But living in Europe and seeing all the churches, great and small, changed some of that for me. The faith of those who'd built them resonated in the walls. Even the most modest houses of God held His presence."

"There's the difference," Katie said. "You were merely visiting churches. Were you ever a member?"

Louis shrugged. "No, I wasn't. Working the restaurant scene didn't allow for Sunday worship. I was usually off on Mondays, and I spent those days sleeping."

"I understand," Katie replied. "I think I'm too jaded about my church experience in Phoenix. Not all churches are gossipy and mean-spirited." For an instant, her eyes filled. "But it sure hurts when they are."

"I can't imagine what Katie Anderson could possibly do to gossip about," Louis said. His gaze was unsettling.

"Just the normal things. Being a single woman, working in an all-male office, in a small suburb. One of my coworkers went through an ugly divorce, and I was presumed to be the cause." She shuddered at the memory. "The fact that his wife left him for another man was ignored. My support for him was interpreted as being involved with him. Never again."

"Never again, what?" Louis asked. "No more churches or no men in your life?"

Katie laughed. Louis was learning way too much

about her and deflecting her need for his students while he did it. Time to refocus the conversation. "No church for now, but I still pray. Lately I pray for culinary arts students to choose my internships. What about it, Louis?"

Raising his hands in surrender, Louis answered, "You're right about a lot of things, Katie. My students could learn loads in a chain setting, and perhaps they'd learn some food prep in addition to budgeting and inventory control. But, and this is a big but, my legitimate fear is they'd be used as substitutes for call-ins. I don't want them to be working the entry stand and giving toddlers crayons to color on the paper table covers."

"Point made," Katie said. "If I could craft a contract for the site managers excluding those things, would that help? There are no sure answers, but the people I've talked to were pretty pumped to give GCC students some experience. What you're missing, Louis, is that our students lend some prestige to the places they'll be working." She paused, slapped the table, and continued. "That's it! We'll make it a condition of the intern name badges that 'GCC Culinary Arts' is listed below their names. Even if they take a little grief from obnoxious folks, it will be a good learning experience."

Louis looked defeated, or possibly just willing to concede this round. It didn't matter to Katie, because she knew she'd broken through some barrier of Louis'. He did that shrug thing again and stood.

"Time for coffee by the fire," he said. "Can you drink caffeine this late?"

"Decaf for me, please," Katie said. "I'm sure you have the perfect beans ready to grind no matter what type of brew you're making."

"You are correct," Louis said. "Come to the kitchen with me while I get things ready."

Katie again marveled at Louis' decor. The kitchen still had an old farmhouse feel, but the restaurant-grade appliances would have been totally out of place next to a farm wife's coffee percolator and icebox. Even the cabinets were a homage to the house's bones. No trendy white shaker boxes for Louis; instead, he'd chosen a chestnut finish that warmed the space without being suffocating. Evidently this man could design as well as cook.

"To repeat myself, your place is gorgeous," she said. "Very upscale but still cozy. Have you ever thought about designing kitchens?"

Louis barked a dismissive laugh. "Not ever, never. Food is my passion. And now, teaching of course. That's why I'm giving you such a hard time, Katie. I don't think you realize how much teaching means to me. It's important that my students graduate from GCC with the best culinary knowledge around."

Katie studied him, wondering how much of that tricky ego fueled his desire to be the best, and to therefore produce the best students. "Isn't it enough to do *your* best, and then admit your students will do what they will with their careers?" she asked. "They have a passion for cooking, simply by virtue of enrolling in your program. But they likely have other passions as well, other motivators besides excelling in a restaurant. I think that's true of all of us; we're motivated by many different things."

Katie knew she wasn't making any headway. It was time to be personal, again, which she hated. "I know there are lots of things important in my life, Louis. My passion at GCC is to mentor students as they sample 'real world' jobs. Supporting that is my goal for them to be smarter than I was about office politics and personalities. But separate from my professional role is my love of my family. Mom and Kristen, baby Michelle and her big sister Sophie—they're my world, whether I'm marketing for internship spots or working as a greeter at a big-box store."

Katie sipped her coffee, which was indeed superb, and ended her speech. "There's lots in this life to be passionate about, Louis. You love your family, and you want the best for your students. But they're allowed to be passionate about their lives, too. If supporting a family with a fast-food managerial job is their choice, that's okay. Right?"

"No, it's not," Louis spat out. "Katie, are you ever quiet? Just enjoy your coffee. Enjoy the fire and our time together. Please."

Katie could take a hint, not that it was much of a hint. Louis made it an order, which was not as off-putting as she expected. He wanted to enjoy the evening. He was trying to make things better between them so they could accomplish their goals at GCC. She relished her drink and enjoyed the fire.

Louis didn't seem to like her silence. This man was tough to please. Katie was determined to obey his command, so she stayed mute.

After gulping a swallow of his coffee, Louis spoke. "How's the decaf?" he asked.

"Wonderful," Katie responded. "As is the fire, which I'm enjoying in silence."

Louis smiled. Katie marveled at the way his eyes lit up when he was genuinely pleased. It happened so rarely, she took note.

"I appreciate this evening, Louis. Dinner was magical, except for the pizza, but I imagine I could grow to like it over time. You really didn't have to do all this. We can work together well without you having to host me every time we disagree." She studied her mug and added, "And you know we'll be fighting regularly, right? But we'll work it out for the benefit of our students."

This time Louis laughed. Not the cynical laugh he so often had, but a real laugh of pleasure. "Fighting with you holds some intrigue, Katie. Peacemaking evenings like this have potential, don't you think?"

Good grief, Katie thought. *He's flirting again.* "Maybe. But more to the point, how can we ensure that we don't argue too much? We need a plan."

"One possibility is that we visit the internship sites I find least objectionable," Louis said. "I can talk to the managers about my concerns, and we could add the idea of making student name badges identify the GCC Culinary Program."

Katie waved her imaginary white flag. If Louis wanted to visit the sites, she'd accompany him to make sure he didn't insult managers with his ridiculous standards. "It's a plan, Louis. I'll share my online schedule with you next week and we'll arrange to visit four or five restaurants. For now, I have to get home. Thanks again for a special evening."

Louis cleaned the kitchen and straightened the living room after Katie left. He wondered about the woman he'd just hosted. Certainly, she was bright, savvy (despite her experience with the church in Phoenix), and hardworking. But it was her passion for her family and those she loved that intrigued him. Most of the women he'd met in Europe were smart, both intellectually and streetwise, but they so often had an agenda related to appearances, what others would think. Family dynamics edged in, but usually for the purpose of influencing the outside world. It struck him as a sad way to live. Katie's focus on her loved ones was refreshing. He had to admit it tapped into something he'd been unable to name when he'd returned to the U.S. He loved his parents and wanted to be with them as they aged. It was that simple and that complex.

Until his interactions with Katie, he'd been a little ashamed of his ties to his parents. The duchess had used her killer intuition and mocked him for being an unsophisticated mama's boy. His coworkers wondered about his priorities, saying that he could surely support his parents financially as they encountered the issues common to cancer and aging. No one understood his ache to be with them, to bond again after so many years.

Katie would get it, though. To her, having a solid relationship with family was as natural as breathing air. He smiled at the thought of her trying to manipulate him into working with her internship program. But perhaps it wasn't entirely manipulative; she hadn't said anything she didn't believe. Her honesty was another thing that attracted him to her.

Aside from her pathetic palate (*had she really said "stinky cheese"?*) there was a lot to be attracted to with Katie Anderson. Her physical attributes (petite frame, mocha-brown eyes, and ivory skin) were what Louis had always considered his type. She was open and forthcoming, unlike the duchess, who always seemed to be hiding her true feelings. No chance of that with Katie. He always knew where he stood with her.

That blasted internship program of hers was

the sticking point in what could be a promising friendship. Laughing to himself, he knew he was lying. Friendship wasn't what came to mind with Katie Anderson. But physical passion alone wasn't it either. Katie was the kind of woman with whom he could have both. The very thought startled him. He had to be careful.

And careful he would be. He had no choice but to go along with Dr. King and allow his students to participate in internship placements. That meant he would be in frequent contact with Katie. No more dinners, either at the cafeteria or in his home. They had to be professional. He had no time or inclination for more evenings like this one. He blew out a frustrated breath as he polished the dining room table. There he was, lying again!

It was time to come clean with himself. No more referring to his previous love as the duchess. Technically, she was an ex-duchess, divorced from her elderly duke. Marie-Christine had meant something to him. He had loved her, even when he realized she wanted him for what amounted to a decorative presence at social events and fun in bed. Why had he taken so long to cut himself free? It seemed odd to thank God for his father's illness, but that's what jolted him back to his Midwestern values. Thank God his father was doing well. What a price to pay for Louis' moral awakening.

Katie entered her house and once again pondered getting a dog so she wouldn't come home to stark silence and reminded herself of the hassles involved with a canine. For now, she was better off living an unencumbered single life. With that burst of wisdom, she was halfway into her pajamas when her phone jingled.

"What is it, Mom?" Katie asked. "Are you okay? It's a little later than you usually call." Katie knew her mother was fine, just trying to find out how the evening with Louis had gone. Kaye's next words confirmed her hunch.

"All is good with me, honey," Kaye said. "How did it go with the award-winning chef? Did you make any headway with your program?"

Kaye was smooth, Katie had to admit. "It went pretty well, Mom. He made a lovely dinner with the exception of an appetizer pizza made with 'stinky cheese.' Can you believe it? I nearly gagged."

"I've had something similar at my old independent-living place in Arizona," Kaye answered. "I think they used Gorgonzola with pears on a pizza-type crust. I pretended to like it, since I was trying to fit in. This one old bitty kept referring to me as the hick from Indiana, so I gave in to peer pressure." She sighed. "At my age, trying to fit in! Who cares? I *am* from Indiana, so there!"

Katie chuckled at the image of her mother feeling that insecure. She understood, however. "Yes, my palate needs some refining, but there are worse problems in life. Anyway, the evening was productive. Louis knows he needs to send students my way, and I agreed to visit some of the potential site restaurants with him so he can speak to the managers. He's the neediest of my faculty members, but I appreciate his concerns."

"Hmmm," Kaye said. "Needy or interested? Sounds to me like he wants to spend time with you."

"He wants to protect his precious students from

going to the dark side of food service. I tried to explain that they could have priorities that include making a living wage after they graduate, but he didn't buy into that. He's a purist about culinary arts."

"Purist, huh? Another word for that is *passionate,* my girl. This Louis Masson could be just what you need." With that, Kaye ended the call.

Katie shrugged and got under her weighted blanket. Yeah, passion was just what she didn't need right now. She had plenty of other challenges to deal with. It was true that she and Dan had lacked some basic passion, but still. Louis was exactly wrong for her. What was her mother thinking? And since they'd made Sunday plans, her mom would have even more time to sing Louis' praises.

Monday dawned crisp and clear, and just as Katie had promised, Louis found a schedule request in his inbox. She must have worked all weekend on this, probably to be sure he wouldn't back down from visiting the potential internship sites with her. He scanned the list of five restaurants with surprise. Sure enough, two were chain eateries. But the other three were members of an Indianapolis group that specialized in different cuisines. Katie had gotten agreements from a steakhouse, a French bistro, and an American-style place that highlighted down-home recipes. The last one even touted "early bird specials," and upon reading that description, Louis realized his parents had spoken fondly of this very restaurant. Just wait until his mom found out his students would be working there. He would have no peace from her constant requests for recipes!

And just as if a clock had chimed, Katie called his office line promptly at nine. "Happy Monday, Louis," she chirped. "Have you checked your email yet?"

"Happy Monday to you also," Louis growled. "How do you manage to be in a good mood this early?" He took a painfully hot swallow of his coffee, choked, and continued. "Yes, I've checked my email. It looks like we're going to be in Indy together all day Thursday. Are you sure you need to go with me? I'm happy to interview the managers on my own."

"Of course, you are," Katie said with false sweetness. "But I insist that you have company. Dr. King wouldn't want there to be any misunderstandings with the managers, right? I figure that between the two of us, we'll iron out all the details, so our students have a seamless transition from the classroom to the world of work."

"You sound like your internship brochure," Louis groused. "And you're really worried I'll offend the contacts you've worked so hard to cultivate. At least be honest, Katie."

After a lengthy pause during which she likely sipped her own coffee, Katie said, "You are correct, Louis. I have worked hard to get these sites in place. There's no way I'm going to let you ruin them for me. Or GCC, for that matter."

Louis had to admire her grit. She was honest to a fault. "Well said, Katie. So, who's driving Thursday? When should we leave?"

It took ten minutes to determine the best way to approach the day, travel times, and driver identification. The last point proved tricky. Katie insisted on driving, since she knew Indianapolis and they were visiting restaurants she had set up. Louis demanded he be the driver, since he would be interviewing the managers and felt the need for a show of influence.

"*Influence?* I think you mean dominance," Katie sputtered. "Perhaps you stayed in Europe too long, Louis. Here in the good old United States of America, women can drive. In fact, we even vote and can have credit cards in our own names. Crazy, huh?"

Louis had to laugh. This woman was funny, most especially when she was annoyed. "I'm driving, Katie. Not because I need to be dominant, but because I want to show you around my old haunts when we're finished with our business. I'll pick you up at seven Thursday morning. We'll clear most of the early rush hour that way."

He ended the call to Katie's continued protests. This was going to be fun. He would have Katie to himself for a whole day away from the GCC campus. He was sure that by day's end they would have argued, laughed, and challenged each other beyond measure. The possibilities were endless.

Chapter Six

Kaye groaned as the shrill chirp of her alarm repeated itself without end. Who in their right mind scheduled a walking club this early in the morning? This was a retirement community, for Pete's sake. It wasn't like most of the walkers had jobs to get to. It was probably just Bob Benson's way of showing how important he was. He'd likely make a point of having crucial meetings to attend.

After shaking off the mental cobwebs and gulping a strong cup of tea, Kaye arrived at the walkers' meeting spot. Bob was there, of course, and so was Linda. She scowled briefly when she saw Kaye, but then recovered and smiled.

"So, you've decided to join us," Linda said, with a questioning look. "I wasn't sure the time would work for you."

"Well, I'm here today," Kaye admitted. "Who knows how long I'll last, especially when the weather turns. My blood is pretty thin after winters in Arizona."

Bob laughed. "You'll be fine, Kaye. Once we hit

freezing temperatures, we meet at the indoor walking track at the fitness club off the interstate. By virtue of living in Gordon Park, you have a membership there."

Linda clutched Bob's arm and said, "Wasn't that brilliant of Bob, to ensure we'd have the ability to stay fit during the winter? He's a peach."

"Yep, a real peach," Kaye said. She turned, grateful, as another member sauntered to their group. At least she wouldn't have to be the odd member of a threesome involving Bob and Linda. Why was life full of such drama? Couldn't she just walk off her fuzzy head and sore joints in peace?

The hour passed pleasantly enough. Kaye enjoyed meeting Margaret, the new member of the group. Bob and Linda were soon several yards ahead of them, which suited her. And Bob would suit Linda, for that matter. They were perfect for each other. Attractive, just a little smug, and very much into appearances. Despite Linda's statement the other day, Bob seemed interested in her.

She must have snorted, because Margaret asked, "What was that Kaye? Is something wrong?"

"No, just stewing about something silly," she replied. "I get too wrapped up in my head sometimes."

"I know just what you mean," Margaret agreed. "When you live alone there's no one to bounce things off of. I do a lot of talking to my dog."

The women laughed and agreed to meet sometime soon for lunch. Kaye returned to her house proud of her efforts and ready for an egg sandwich. Her doorbell rang, and she assumed Linda was checking in to gauge Kaye's feelings for Bob.

As she suspected, her visitor was Linda, but not

for the reason she'd thought. "Kaye, you've got to hear what Bob just told me. Do you know why we walk so early?"

"He's probably got to save the world or something," Kaye said. She hated her unkindness and wondered what it meant. She wasn't usually this mean. And wasn't she trying to forgive him?

"No, he's working on saving *himself*," Linda said. "His diabetes is out of control despite the weight he's lost. So, he has a support group right after our walks, then he goes to a diabetes clinic in Indy to learn about his new insulin pump. He's wearing a medical alert necklace since his blood sugars fluctuate so much."

Now she really did feel guilty. Bob was fighting a serious illness and she'd ignored that possibility. "Gosh, I'm sorry to hear that, Linda. He looks so healthy. I had no idea."

"Neither did I," Linda said. "The last thing I need right now is a sick man in my life. Been there, done that." She sipped the tea Kaye had provided and looked at her immaculately manicured fingernails. "He's all yours, Kaye. He's a nice guy, but I've got a life to live. Watching someone suffer again isn't a part of my plan."

Kaye was dumbfounded into silence which, as both of her daughters would have attested had they been present, never happened. She finally recovered and said, "I can relate to what you're saying, Linda. My Stan was ill with cancer before he died of a heart condition. But you can be friends with Bob, can't you? From what I've read, there are lots of good treatments for diabetes now."

"Yes, friends it is. But I'd planned on more until I

heard what he said today. I've got to get going, Kaye. Thanks for the tea."

Closing the door after Linda's exit, Kaye made her breakfast sandwich but enjoyed it less than she'd imagined she would. A tear snaked down her cheek. Why was she crying? Was she actually sorry that Bob was sick? Maybe it was just the memories of Stan's illness. Grief sometimes surfaced at odd times.

Her doorbell sounded again, and she wiped her eyes. It wasn't even ten and she was welcoming her second visitor. This 55+ community was busy!

Bob Benson stood on her porch. He smiled and said, "Hi again. Can I come in?"

"Sure, Bob. I just finished breakfast, but I'd be glad to make you something if you haven't eaten."

"No, I ate after we walked," he answered. "I wouldn't refuse a cup of coffee, though." He smiled as he spoke, and Kaye was struck by the sadness behind his eyes.

After the coffee was brewed, they sat in the living area with their respective drinks. Bob shifted in his seat, took a drink, and blurted, "I saw Linda make a beeline for your place after we all walked. Did she inform you about my health issues?"

Kaye shrugged and figured honesty was best. "She did, Bob. I felt it was your story to tell, so I didn't say much to her. I'm sorry you're struggling." Kaye looked at him, again surprised that she felt something, maybe compassion, for this man who had treated Kristen so badly. "If I can help in any way, let me know."

"Thank you, Kaye. There might be a time I'll need a ride to Indianapolis or help with picking up meds. I'll let you know." He paused and said, "The reason I stopped by was to defuse what Linda might have told you. I've had diabetes for years, with good success at managing my health. As I've aged, things have changed. I'm just tweaking my treatment."

Laughing, Kaye nodded in agreement. "Believe me, I know about 'tweaking treatment.' I'm not diabetic, but I've got other ailments. Comes with the territory, I guess. Who knows? I might need your help in the future as well. We can be each other's health-care buddies."

Bob sighed and laced his fingers together. "There's more," he said. "This latest setback has me thinking too much. I can't help worrying that God is punishing me for my past. I was a good husband and father, but at work I could be arrogant. As you're well aware, Kristen paid for my bad character choices. God is getting my attention by damaging my health. Maybe I'm paying for past sins."

Kaye wished she'd paid more attention to the church sermons in Phoenix. The pastor at her old church had addressed this very theme more than once. She decided to give it her best. "Bob, I'm not sure God works that way. Yes, we need to take responsibility for our actions, but I doubt God metes out punishment in the way you believe." Another tear made its way down her cheek, but she ignored it. "My Stan was a good man through and through. But he suffered terribly with his cancer and then left us when our lives were getting back to normal. That wasn't God's punishment...it was just the result of our imperfect world and time's effect on our human bodies. That probably makes no sense to you, but it's what I believe."

Bob put his mug on the side table, stood, and was next to her before she knew what was happening. After a big hug, he said, "Thanks for that, Kaye. You're a good woman. Maybe I should talk to my pastor about all this." Taking his coat and hat, he opened the door and said, "And to make things even worse, Linda had me in the grave by the end of the week. She's full of drama, you know?"

As promised, at seven on Thursday morning, Louis was beeping his horn outside Katie's house. She piled into the car and glared. "Maybe if you'd honked a few more times, the whole neighborhood would have been awakened. Rude, Louis."

"Sorry," he replied. "I wasn't thinking. I hope your neighbors are already up for school or work."

Katie had to be honest. "Most of them are, in fact. Perhaps my gripe was more about being summoned like a girl on a date with an arrogant guy." She winked and said, "It all fits, you know?"

Louis huffed and drove to the I-70 entrance ramp. "I resent that, but you're right. In Europe we walked everywhere. I've lost my polish when it comes to driving."

"Let's hope you remember how to navigate city traffic," Katie answered. "In the meantime, I'll fill you in on the managers we're meeting with today."

The hour on the interstate was spent review-ing the internship slots they were to visit and the backgrounds of the managers involved. Katie em-phasized that two of the four had culinary training.

She wasn't about to let Louis condescend to hard-working Indiana folks.

Studying his profile, she was again impressed by his looks. He could have been a film star, or a glamorous celebrity chef. Why was he in Indiana? Since he was captive behind the wheel, Katie decided to take the risk and ask.

"Apart from your dad's illness, which I'm glad to hear is being successfully treated, what led you back to the U.S.? Is it what you'd hoped it would be?"

Donning his usual scowl, Louis passed a slow-moving truck. "It was time, Katie. I like seeing my parents more often. GCC is what I expected. In a few more semesters, it will be what I hoped."

Such arrogance! Katie literally bit her tongue before she shot back. *Relax, girl*, she thought. *Use this opportunity to learn more about this man. You'll be dealing with him a lot, so knowledge is power.*

"I understand about timing, Louis," she said softly. "Mom and I were ready to come back, but we were afraid to tell each other. Moving to Phoenix wasn't a mistake but staying there would have been."

"Well put, Katie. I loved Europe, England especially, but I was finished."

Katie's usual pause didn't yield any more from Louis, so she had to ask more questions. "What was it that tipped your decision? For me, it was the unlivable summer weather and the ache of not seeing Kristen and her growing family. Plus, the situation at work and church, which you've heard about."

"Lots of things factored in for me," Louis said. "Cost of living, all that."

Pausing again, Katie waited Louis out.

"Okay, it was a woman," he finally said. "We had an intense relationship but very different life goals." Louis turned to look at Katie, warning her with his glare. "No more questions, okay?"

Katie nodded and soon they were at the first restaurant. "Let's do this, Louis. I'll stay quiet and let you ask about the experiences your students will have."

Louis looked relieved and behaved well throughout all the visits. Katie was surprised at his easy manner with the managers, his knowledge of convenience foods used in a restaurant setting, and his appreciation of the challenges of leading a staff with lots of turnover. More importantly, Louis' consideration of the line staff and waiters was special. He even had lengthy talks with the people working the host stands.

As they walked to the car after the last interview, she said, "That was great, Louis. I learned so much from your questions. I think the managers felt valued, too. You're quite the diplomat when you choose to be."

Laughing hard, Louis unlocked the car. "Shocked you, huh?"

"Yes, you did," Katie admitted. "Lunch is my treat. Where to?"

"We're eating at my parents' house. Mom has country ham sandwiches and potato salad for us," Louis said. Seeing Katie's wide eyes, he added, "She insisted. When she found out I was going to be in town, she made lunch a mandatory event. Mom isn't a chef, but we'll have a good meal. Her potato salad is a recipe I've used a time or two in London for Americana-themed events."

Wonders never ceased. Katie was going to meet Louis' mother.

Kaye dressed carefully, easing into fashionable jeans and a swirly top embroidered with tiny flowers. Her ankle boots completed her look, though she was befuddled as to the reason for her concern about her appearance. She was about to have lunch with Rose Dolce, a woman she'd known forever. They had daughters of similar ages, and Rose was a good person. Kind, authentic, and giving. But Rose had another side to her. When crossed, or even questioned, she could be tough. Her daughter, Annie, had developed into a fine woman as well, though it took leaving Rose's home for her to come into her own. Kaye understood and sent a silent prayer up to the Lord that she was less interfering with her daughters than her friend was.

Maybe her anxiety was related to all the newness that the move back to Gordon had entailed. She was thrilled to be here, but things had changed. What had she expected? That things would remain the same, lives untouched by the passage of time? Of course, people moved on with their lives!

Entering the restaurant located in the middle of Gordon's main street, she wasn't surprised to see Rose had gotten there first. She waved to her friend and joined her at the table.

"I've ordered your iced tea," Rose announced. "They've got some fruity blend today in addition to the usual black tea. And the special of the day is a Monte Christo sandwich." Rose looked pleased at having taken control.

Kaye grinned at her friend and said, "Thanks, Rose. It's so good to see you. I've missed our luncheon chats. Phone calls aren't the same, are they?"

"No, not at all," Rose said. "I'm glad you and Katie came to your senses and returned to Gordon." Catching herself, she added, "I'm sorry. That was unkind. I understand why you felt you had to leave. Losing Stan was terrible. How are you doing, Kaye?"

This was the friend Kaye missed, kind and loving Rose. "I'm well, thanks. My house in Gordon Park is almost decorated to my liking. I'll have you over next week for a meal and a tour." She sipped her tea, relishing the subtle taste of peach. "My only major adjustment is living in what amounts to a group setting. Everyone is in each other's business. As Kristen would say, I need to set some boundaries."

Rose nodded knowingly. "Yes, you're all on top of each other with those small lots. Everyone's retired with nothing much to do. But you'll figure it out, Kaye. You have a full life. Tell me about your neighbors."

Kaye told Rose about Linda, which led to a discussion of Bob and his health. "I'm truly sorry he's ill, but according to him, it's all being managed. I was surprised Linda was so put off by it all."

Rose's eyes narrowed and Kaye knew she was in for some serious pontificating.

"Well, Linda could have a point," Rose said. "Bob's health could take a turn anytime. You know what they say, right?"

Kaye had no clue what "they" might be saying. She shook her head.

"The standard advice for dating at our age is, 'Don't be a nurse or a purse.' You've already suffered through Stan's cancer and heart attack. Why put yourself through that again?"

Kaye was appalled. "Rose, Bob and I are just friends, and barely that. I still don't trust him completely, despite his apologies about what he did to Kristen. It's no big deal. We're just in a walking group together."

Rose tapped her chin. "You'll see, Kaye. He'll be stopping by more and more. He'll ask for rides to the doctor, and to pay you back he'll take you out for a nice dinner. You'll be dating before you know it."

"Dating!" Kaye squeaked. "Rose, we're not going to date!"

Rose's dark eyes flashed. "Someone is protesting a bit too much," she said. "Plus, if he asks for help with his medical bills, run like the wind. You need to take care of yourself and preserve your inheritance for your girls."

"My inheritance!" Kaye sputtered. "Rose, you've got me with one foot in the grave. It's just a walking club, truly."

Sensing she'd done her duty by her innocent friend, Rose changed the subject as they dug into their warm sandwiches. "How are your girls, by the way?"

Kaye filled Rose in about Kristen's daughters and Katie's job at GCC. The rest of the meal passed uneventfully, which Kaye thanked God for. She loved Rose but being with her was exhausting.

Louis pulled into the driveway of a bungalow in Speedway, Indiana. "This is my parents' place, since before I was born," he announced. "They love Speedway. It's a small town in terms of autonomy but is actually encapsulated by the greater Indianapolis area. Of course, the summer months are hectic with the Indy 500 and other races, but they seem to enjoy that, too."

He smiled at the memories the house sparked. "If you really want to know about my love of all things related to food service, look no further than the racetrack. I started serving popcorn there when I was fifteen."

They hadn't gotten three steps out of the car when a smiling, silver-haired woman greeted them from the porch. "Louis honey, it's so good to see you!" she said. "What a treat to have you here twice in one week. After all those years in Europe, Dad and I didn't think we'd ever have a consistent relationship again." She walked to meet them at the car.

Louis rolled his eyes and kissed his mother. "Mom, this is Katie Anderson, a coworker of mine at GCC. We've been visiting internship sites for my students, as I told you on the phone."

Katie tried to shake the older woman's hand but was enveloped in a warm embrace. "Nice to meet you, Mrs. Masson," she said. "I hope we're not imposing."

"Just call me Evelyn, please. My husband, Bradley, awaits us inside. I've got him slicing the ham. Nothing but the best for my chef son, but I fear we fall short most of the time."

Unable to stop himself, the eye rolls continued, and Louis felt a headache coming on. "Mom, cut it out. You know you've made this ham and its special glaze since I was five. Katie is aware I'm a chef, and that I've worked in Europe. No need to impress her." *Like it's even possible,* he thought. The most impressive thing he'd done with Katie was to treat the staff members respectfully this morning, which indicated how low her expectations were of him.

Katie seemed to enjoy Evelyn's coy manner. Louis couldn't understand why, but the two women got along well. He moved from the living room to the kitchen to help his father, who had good color but was still too thin for Louis' liking.

"How are things going, Dad?" he asked.

"Very well, son. The doc gave me several gold stars when he got my lab results back. And I've been going to the spin class at the gym twice a week. Building muscle, as they say."

Louis surveyed his father's baggy slacks and loose shirt. "That's great, Dad. But I think you need to focus on increasing your calories. Add some fat to your entrees and eat that evening ice cream to your heart's content."

The foursome enjoyed their lunch at the kitchen table, laughing about Louis' high jinks as a young boy and his eventual journey to Culver Academy. Louis was again shocked at Katie's ease with his mother and father. Why was this woman pleased with everyone but him? He loved his parents, but they were typical comfortable boomers—relaxed in their retirements, firm to rigid in their beliefs, and sure of the way the world should work. He'd been on the receiving end of their judgments many times. Of course, they were also dealing with his dad's illness, but his prognosis was good.

Later, as they made their way to I-465, Louis decided to voice his questions. Katie looked startled, almost alarmed. "Why do I like your parents? Are you serious? They're fine people, they've suffered a lot lately, and they were welcoming to me. Some folks would have resented my presence, you know."

"Yeah, yeah," Louis muttered. "But you accepted them at face value, without wondering what agenda they might have. You've never done that with me."

Katie whipped her head around and grabbed his arm, almost causing him to swerve into the next lane. "I've done everything to accept you, Louis. You've been the one to keep me at arm's length, ignoring my calls, and viewing my internships as time-wasters."

Louis knew she was right, but he had to make his point. "All true, but you've never accepted my concerns as valid. You've categorized me as elitist because I want to educate quality chefs."

Silence greeted his statement. After fifteen minutes, Katie finally spoke. "You may have a point. The label 'elitist' could have crossed my mind a time or two. You even pronounce your name in the French fashion, which you have to admit is pretty unusual for a Speedway guy. But when I tried to tell you our students could need jobs after graduation that paid well, that didn't seem to matter to you."

Louis gripped the steering wheel. "Pay matters, Katie. Jobs matter. But so does quality."

After Louis dropped her off, Katie shed her professional clothes and welcomed the comfort of her joggers and T-shirt. What a day. Louis had been alternately charming, knowledgeable, vulnerable, stuffy, and a good son. She noticed the concern in his eyes when he saw his dad's loose clothing. Katie had also been aware of his parents' almost pitiful gratitude for his presence in their lives. There were stories with that little family, but she doubted she'd ever learn them.

Still full from lunch, Katie had a cup of soup as she watched an old movie. Her thoughts wandered to Louis' interactions with the restaurant staff members. To be that comfortable, that empathetic, he had to have worked in every position a restaurant offered. Blushing, she had to admit she'd sold him short. Louis Masson was more than a gorgeous guy and a French name. His passion for his students made more sense now, but he needed to realize that GCC wasn't the Culinary Institute of America. Their students needed to make a living for themselves and often for their families.

Chapter Seven

True to his word, Louis sent six students to Katie's office the following week for orientation prior to starting their internships. She reviewed the expectations for their time on the job, the format of the weekly reports they would submit to her and Louis, and the importance of maintaining a professional stance when they were at work. "There's no horsing around, got it? View your placement as the first culinary job you'll ever have. If you do well, the contacts you make could lead to better, full-time jobs after graduation. Any questions?"

The usual queries followed concerning work attire, how to handle sick days, and whether to call Katie or Louis if a problem occurred. "Call me first," she answered. "I'll decide if Chef Masson needs to be notified. We don't want to bother him if we don't have to."

The students nodded seriously, agreeing that Chef M, as they referred to him, was too important to be bothered with trifles like a minor fever. Katie was astounded at their respect for, or possibly fear of, Louis. *He's almost brainwashed them, and I understand.* His tactics with her had actually made her nervous about her job stability.

The students left the meeting but one lingered. "Ms. Anderson, do you have a minute?" Sarah asked.

Katie liked Sarah, a nontraditional student about her own age. Katie knew she was a single parent of one little girl, living on student loans and not much else. "What can I help you with, Sarah?" she asked.

"It's not really me," Sarah hedged. "Did you know there are other students in our program who would like to do an internship?"

Nonplussed, Katie was startled. "No, my understanding was that the six of you were it for this semester. There are others?"

"I know of at least three more. Chef Masson told them there weren't enough suitable internship sites to accommodate them. I got the impression from you today that you could find other restaurants if needed. Maybe Chef M didn't understand."

Oh, he understands all right. Katie understood, too. "Yes, that must be it, Sarah. Thanks for filling me in. I'll give Chef M a call later today." *After I cool down.*

Sarah left for her next class and Katie planned her strategy with Louis. He obviously knew the remaining restaurants in her list of sites were all chains, the majority being fast-food spots. She thought she'd convinced him there were valid experiences to be had at those places, but he'd fooled her. Her face flamed at the thought that at least three students were being denied the chance to gain real food-service experience due to Louis and his prejudices. They were also being denied the chance to earn some money, since the grant Katie had written allowed students to be paid more than minimum wage for their internship time. Didn't Louis realize many GCC students were strapped for cash? Sarah was a prime example. She told Katie straight up that the internship would pay for her weekly food costs.

Knowing she was in no frame of mind to speak to Louis yet, Katie reflected on the rest of her program. Students had been placed in several internships. Some were in health-care settings, some in retail, a few in IT, and the rest in various small businesses in Gordon and communities close by. For the most part, things were going well. Based on the reports Katie read religiously each week and on the phone updates she received from internship site managers, GCC students were doing themselves proud.

She was doing herself proud, too. Dr. King had set a first semester goal for her of thirty sites. She currently had students in forty-two spots. Three more from Louis would make a tidy forty-five.

Her efforts to calm herself weren't working. It was after five and Katie was ready to call the day over. A knock on her door prevented that.

Louis let himself in and smiled. "Headed out? I was on my way also, and I thought we could get some dinner together while we discussed your meeting with my students today."

"I think not," Katie answered. "The meeting went well until I discovered you've been holding out on me. My day is done. We can talk later. Thanks." She turned and locked her office. She made it to the parking lot, but Louis blocked her car door.

"Holding out on you? What do you mean? Stay here and confront me like an adult."

"Fine. I've been informed that an additional three more of your students desire internships, but you've told them there are none available. The *adult* response would have been for you to tell them about the sites I still have. Again, the elitist in you won't allow them to work in a fast-food setting, despite all the valuable things they could learn about staffing, budgeting, and customer service." Katie jerked her front door open and shoved Louis out of her way. "Hold on. We've had this conversation already. Why am I repeating myself?"

Louis' face resembled the college founder's granite statue at the entrance to GCC. He turned and Katie was barely able to hear his reply. "I will not have my students asking customers if they want fries with their burger. That's not elitist, Katie. It's being a good educator."

Katie called Kristen on her drive home. She needed some sisterly advice, and maybe a psychologist's take on Louis' narcissistic issues. Kristen told her to come straight to her home for dinner. As luck would have it, Mike and Sophie were out having pizza. Baby Michelle was down for the night.

After pouring out the story over leftovers and two glasses of wine, Katie looked expectantly at Kristen. "Well, what do you think? He's a self-centered mess, right? How am I going to handle him?"

Kristen sipped her own wine and studied her sister. Speaking slowly, she said, "You've asked me three questions. Let's start with what I think. You're not going to like it."

Katie could feel the heat rise to her cheeks. "Go

ahead."

"I think you and Louis are the perfect definition of a classic battle for control. You're both strong-willed, used to getting your own way, and uninterested in what the other really thinks."

Still hot, but willing to hear Kristen out, Katie repeated, "Go ahead."

"Secondly, he's self-centered, but so are you when it comes to your job. Dr. King won't care if you have forty-two or forty-five slots filled. He'll be tickled pink that you've made a success of the program either way. Am I correct?"

"Maybe," Katie said with a shrug. "But what about the students who want to have a placement this semester?"

"That leads me to your last question," Kristen said, clearing their plates. "Before we talk about how to handle Louis, let's look at the desserts I've stashed away from Sophie. That kid eats all my treats if I don't hide them."

After choosing two large pieces of dark chocolate with their coffee, Kristen resumed her advice. "First, let go of the need to 'handle' Louis. Treat him like the award-winning professional he is, one with values and priorities for his program. You need to *listen,* Katie. Sure, those three extra students could use the money your placements would provide, but at what real cost? Would they learn much frying burgers and ordering the limited inventory items required?"

Katie gave her sister a glare, almost stood to leave, but sat down again. Letting the last remnants of chocolate dissolve in her mouth, she said, "Thanks, Sis. I'm not sure I agree with your points, but I'm glad you've made them. I won't talk to Louis until I've thought things through."

Hugging her sister, Katie went to her car and drove the short distance home. Thinking things through took most of her night.

Louis looked at his office phone with disgust. Katie was calling again and refusing to leave a voicemail. He knew this was due to his previous pattern of ignoring messages from her, but he still ignored her call. They were at an obvious impasse. She had him pegged as a snob. He viewed her as a woman so full of ambition that she refused to remember they were in the profession of education, not fast-food service. He had compromised on the six restaurants she found for his students. He refused to bend further. He wasn't totally ignorant of his students' financial needs; just last week he'd sent a struggling sophomore to the combined campus food pantry and clothes closet. And he was generous with his job recommendations, even for those jobs in greasy burger joints. He didn't care if students worked in those places, but he sure wasn't going to endorse them for academic credit.

He realized his food lab started in a few minutes and hustled to gather his teaching materials. Today's lab, unlike the one Katie had attended, focused entirely on the cuts of beef. He'd convinced a local butcher to bring a butchered and wrapped side of beef and, via a YouTube video Louis had vetted, demonstrate how it became filets, sirloins, stew meat, and hamburger. Louis had financed the entire cost and planned to distribute the cuts of meat to the students after class. In addition, the butcher was going to discuss the benefits of grass-fed versus corn-fed beef, a topic probably tantamount to blasphemy in corn-heavy Indiana.

Entering the food lab, he was glad to see students huddled around the butcher and the demonstration table. Louis started the computer and displayed a graphic of a side of beef with the various cuts and their location on the large screen at the front of the room. He introduced his guest speaker, Fred Banning, and moved to the back of the lab, which he had darkened except for the screen. He wanted his students to focus on the video demonstration with no distractions.

The video began and Fred, enjoying the limelight which probably was scarce for a meat cutter, stopped it periodically to share his own comments and observations. The video cut to a picture of the organ meats including the heart, liver, and intestines, which had already been removed from the carcass. Louis heard a thud behind him. None of the people in the front of the dark room noticed.

Katie was on the floor, looking distinctly green. She muttered something about "blood and guts" and tried to get up. Louis scooped her into his arms and walked out to the rear hallway. "This is certainly a dramatic way to get my attention," he drawled. "I'd have called you back in a few days."

He sat Katie on a bench in the hall, saw the bottle of water in her bag, and offered her a sip. After a few seconds, she was fine. Or as fine as this contentious woman could be.

"Thanks for the rescue, Louis," she said. "You're right. I came here because I knew you'd have to talk to me after your lab. Unfortunately, I didn't know you'd be having the equivalent of a Halloween haunted house as your special learning experience today. God help your students."

He couldn't help himself. His laugh echoed down the empty hallway, and he relished the sight of Katie Anderson looking sweaty and off-color. Despite her frazzled state, she was as cute as ever. He had a flash of memory of Marie-Christine after a night of heavy partying. Hungover and nauseated, she had resembled Katie's current state. But Marie-Christine had *not* been a bit cute. Nor had she been funny or self-deprecating. Katie had the generosity of spirit to be both.

Beyond her sweetness, Louis was surprised at how pleasant carrying Katie had been. Her figure was slight but firm. She was a fit woman, though not at the level of her sister, Kristen, who ran marathons. Katie's build was softer, rounder. He liked that and had a fleeting image of what her body would be like under more pleasant circumstances. *Time to center, fella.*

"Give me fifteen minutes," he said. "Stay here and take deep breaths. I'll wind up in the lab, give my speaker his honorarium, and be back soon."

"I'm not going anywhere," Katie said as she pressed her cheek on the cool concrete block wall behind the bench. "This is my cozy place."

Louis returned after twenty minutes. "Sorry, Katie. The students had lots of questions and then I had to hand out the meat. How are you doing?"

"I'm much better, except for being mortified. I hope I didn't disrupt your class."

"Not at all. The meat saws in the video presentation made so much noise you weren't noticed. I directed everyone to leave out the front door of the classroom, which was very kind of me, if I do say so myself."

Katie frowned. "It was, and I appreciate it. Now you know my secret. There's a reason I'm not a doctor or a nurse. I can't even watch when I get my own blood drawn." She inhaled and took another sip of her water. "Did you just say you gave the students all that meat? Did your speaker donate his beef?"

"Hardly. I donated the cost of the beef to the college, specifically to my students. Despite what you think, I do know our students have financial pressures. It's not a big deal."

"I'm an Indiana girl, Louis. I know what a side of beef goes for. That was very generous."

"Thank you," he said. Curious, he asked, "Are you able to cook with this aversion to blood and guts? How do you feed yourself?"

Now it was Katie's turn to laugh. "Good question. I simply convince myself that if the meat or chicken comes in a tidy package, wrapped in clear plastic and neatly labeled, it has nothing to do with a real animal. You could say I turn it into an abstract thing, one that will nourish me and those I love."

"Whatever works for you," Louis said. "I'm glad to hear you're not a vegan." Noticing the glare coming in his direction, he backtracked. "Not that there's anything wrong with vegans or vegetarians or pescatarians." He blew a frustrated sigh. "I value their commitment to the health of themselves and the earth. But they sure miss out on a lot of good eating."

"True, though you'd never convince them of that. Kristen flirts with being a vegetarian, but then caves when she wants a steak." Katie stood and straightened her rumpled clothing. "Now that I've got you at my disposal, I don't have the energy to talk. I guess we'll have to do this some other day."

Louis admitted to himself that Katie did look tired. Working a full day and then passing out on the food lab floor would do that to a person. He decided to have pity on her, but knew he was also unwilling to cause her more distress. Something in him regretted his part in her job challenges. "I agree. Here's a thought. Call me around nine tomorrow morning, and I promise to answer. Should I prepare for another Katie Anderson essay on why my students should be allowed to take any internship they want?"

Throwing her large tote bag over her shoulder, Katie shook her head. "No, I wasn't going to do the talking. I'm ready to listen."

Mortified, Katie changed into her flannel pajamas the second she was in her bedroom. She buried her head under her down pillow and breathed hard. What a goof she must seem to Louis. Passing out during his lab! And not a live lab, a video! But such were the Anderson sensibilities. Her mom and sister were the same. None of them could handle blood, vomit, or any other body secretions. Kristen even had trouble changing Michelle's diapers for the first few weeks of the baby's life. Too bad Chef "Lewis" Masson had to witness her weakness.

Secretly, she enjoyed calling Louis by the anglicized pronunciation of his name, if only in her head. She knew she'd better stop before she said it out loud during one of their arguments. They had plenty of other things to argue about and making fun of his name wasn't at all in line with Kristen's advice to listen and honor Louis' passion for his career and students.

Did she really honor Louis' devotion to his students? Didn't her devotion to them matter? They needed to learn, they needed money, and thanks to her grant she could help meet both needs.

What about his donation of an entire side of beef? That was certainly an indication of his love of his students. Had she underestimated Louis? Did he care about GCC as much as she did?

Plus, she had to admit he'd been kind to her. He'd nursed her after her fainting episode and spared her of being exposed to his students in her frazzled state. He was also very strong, picking her up as if she weighed only a few pounds. She had quite liked it, feeling enveloped by his muscular arms and firm trunk, except for being nauseated and clammy at the same time.

What would it be like if they were friends and not adversaries? Despite his Indiana roots, he looked European, almost exotic, with his dark looks, brooding glances, and artful use of his hands when he cooked. She wondered what his hands would be like if put to other uses. Blushing, she rolled over and tried to sleep.

The next morning Katie dressed with care, drank her usual three cups of strong coffee, and headed to her office. Promptly at nine, she dialed Louis' extension. He answered on the second ring.

"Very punctual, Katie," he said. "What did you mean when you said you wanted to listen? I'm confused."

"Understandably," she said. "We need to meet in person for this. What's your schedule like today?"

"I'm free after two. Until then I've got back-to-back classes and meetings."

"If you can delay your lunch until then, I'll treat. I still owe you from your mom's wonderful meal."

"You don't owe me anything," Louis groused. "I'll meet you in your office at two."

True to his word, Louis arrived on time. Katie packed her tote with her laptop and a few files of papers to grade. "What's your pleasure for lunch, Louis?"

"You're the host. You can decide."

"Fine. Follow me in your car, since it sounds like we're both finished for the day. We're headed to Mac's Diner in New Castle. It will only take about fifteen minutes."

Louis nodded in agreement, clearly puzzled at Katie's agenda.

At the diner, they ordered, and Katie again took charge. "I meant what I said yesterday, Louis. Kristen convinced me I haven't been listening to you. I realize you have a true love of your profession and your students. Help me understand why internships at the burger joints are so offensive to you."

Louis hunched his shoulders, seemingly frustrated at another wasted attempt to educate Katie. "I believe my students are placed in internship settings to learn, Katie. The restaurants we visited in Indianapolis will provide great learning opportunities. Typical chains won't, though they do pay relatively well. They also give students a sense of the demands of food service—the hours, the staffing challenges, and the difficulties of dealing with the public."

He shifted as the waiter brought their food. "That said, you should also know that I've helped several of my students get part-time jobs at those places. They're working out well and have validated my concerns. One kid told me last week his most recent shift had consisted of mopping the floors for four hours straight. He cleaned the kitchen, the dining area, and the bathrooms. It's great work experience, but not internship caliber." He munched on his salad and almost pleaded his case. "Don't you see my point, Katie?"

Katie's own salad seemed stuck in her throat. Taking a big gulp of her iced tea, she said, "I do see, Louis. You've helped me understand, which is what I asked. I'm sorry it took me so long."

Louis looked at Katie with round eyes, though she was again distracted by their intense color and sparkle. She tried to compose herself and continued her semi-prepared speech. "I guess we're not that different. We both care about our students, we want them to learn as much as they possibly can, and we realize they have challenging lives outside the classroom."

"All true, Katie. But our methods diverge from our shared sentiments. Right?"

"That's been true up to now," Katie admitted. "But I agree that mopping floors is no learning experience. How can we meet in the middle? How can our students have more internship options without wasting their time on mundane tasks?"

"My, my," Louis said. "Who's sounding elitist now? After all, restaurants won't be open if they're not clean."

Angry that her attempts at finding peace were being turned against her, Katie said, "Quit twisting my words, Louis. In fact, you were the one who just said mopping floors wasn't a quality learning experience." She shook her head. "You're mocking me. What's that about?"

"I'm not mocking you," Louis said, taking her hand across the table. "You've tried to find some middle ground between us, but it's not going to happen beyond the six restaurants I've approved. Give it up, Katie."

Give it up? That was it. Katie was finished. She freed her hand from Louis' and rose. Her half-eaten salad (which was a fresh Caesar, loaded with Parmesan shavings, tender grilled chicken strips, and four fat anchovies) was too good to leave. She signaled the waitress and after boxing her meal said, "I understand, Chef M. This semester's culinary arts internships are complete. As always, it's been a pleasure, *Lewis.*"

Turning on her heel before she came to the door of the diner, she added, "I sure hope that side of beef gets those students through the rest of the semester. If not, reconsider sending them to me. I'll find them an internship spot for general studies or business credit that will help them get through the holidays. Your name and precious reputation won't be tarnished, trust me."

Chapter Eight

Kaye couldn't understand how it happened, but she and Bob were the only walkers most mornings. Linda wasn't there, which was no surprise. The other members of the walking club had assorted excuses that could be translated to the lack of desire to get up so early to walk in the brisk autumn air. Usually, Kaye didn't want to leave her snuggly covers, but she knew Bob needed the exercise to help manage his diabetes. And the exercise would benefit her sore joints.

As their paces became synchronous, Kaye struggled to make conversation. Bob was unusually quiet today. Tiring of the silence, she decided the direct approach was best.

"What's going on, Bob?" she asked. "Do you want to cut the walk short today?"

"Nothing's wrong, Kaye. I'm grateful for your company. I could use a rest, though. My stamina isn't good lately."

Fifty yards down the path was a bench, usually occupied by two Gordon Park residents who were having a secret flirtation, unknown to either of their spouses. Today it was empty, thankfully. Kaye directed Bob to the bench and sat next to him.

"We're in luck," she said. "The two lovebirds aren't here."

"There's a sad story there," Bob said, easing into the backrest. "Each of them has a spouse with severe dementia. I'm not saying what they're doing is right, but it is understandable."

Kaye's face reddened. "There I go again, judging others! I try to stop, but it sneaks up on me. I'm truly sorry for my assumptions."

"No worries, Kaye. After you've lived here a while, you'll realize we're all of an age to have histories filled with regrets, a backlog of mistakes, and the propensity to make new ones. We're human, after all." He sipped from his insulated thermos of coffee and added, "God is on our side, no matter what we do, right?"

Smiling, Kaye agreed and patted his hand. "Thanks be to God," she said. "His forgiveness never ends."

Bob took the opportunity to lace his fingers with hers. "This is nice, Kaye. It reminds me of time with my wife, before she got sick. I miss having a companion, a partner in life." He looked at her and winked. "I even miss romance. What about you?"

Flushing even more, Kaye took a deep breath. Eager for a distraction, she noticed the small monitor-type gadget clipped to Bob's coat pocket. Pointing to it, she asked, "What's that, Bob? I've never seen a cell phone like that."

"It's not a phone," Bob replied. "My kids got it for me, much to my chagrin. It's a medical monitoring device so I can get help if I need it. The 'base camp' has all my medical info, and the unit has a GPS tracking system." He sighed and patted the device. "Pretty pathetic, huh?"

Another wave of sadness fluttered through Kaye. Why did aging have to be like this? Three steps back for every step forward, and with outsiders monitoring every move? Maybe Stan was the lucky one. He'd have hated growing old. Kaye's faith wavered at times, but she was sure she would be reunited with Stan in heaven when the time was right. That was a comfort of sorts. Remembering Bob was waiting on her reply, she said, "Your kids love you a lot, Bob. Even though you're surrounded by others here, they want to be sure you're safe."

She squeezed his hand. "And are you safe, Bob? Not in the conventional sense, because I know you are, but what about the day-to-day things? Do you cook?"

Bob grinned and let go of her hand. "Don't turn all mother hen on me, Kaye. You'd be surprised at all the advances in frozen microwavable dinners today. I'm looking forward to a fried chicken dinner tonight, complete with mashed potatoes, corn, and a brownie. I eat like a king."

Kaye was caught by her sudden sympathy for this lonely man. "Frozen dinners, huh? They're okay on occasion, but not every night." She tapped her finger on her chin. "We've got to do something about this, Bob. You're not the only person in Gordon Park who fights the decision about what to have for dinner each evening." Suddenly inspired, she stood. "I've got it! We need a dinner club!"

"A dinner club?" Bob asked. "I don't follow. What I do follow is that you're dodging my comment about wanting a little romance in my life." He looked at Kaye with sad eyes. "I didn't mean to offend. Just tell me to back off if I'm too much."

Unsettled, Kaye debated about whether she should be honest. Why not? She'd just asked God for continued forgiveness and lying to Bob would seem to be counterproductive. "You didn't offend me. I agree about missing companionship. Stan and I had shared history, the experience of being poor newlyweds, stories about parenting the girls, living through the deaths of our parents, and on and on." Kaye smiled at a cardinal as he flew by, landing on a naked branch. Maybe it was a sign that Stan was nearby. "We even communicated at times with movie lines that fit the moment. *Captain Ron,* hardly a classic, was one of our favorites."

Kaye almost shuddered as the memories threatened to bring tears. "Those times were so precious," she said. "But romance? I'm not ready for that. Not sure if I'll ever be." The thought of being intimate with a man other than Stan was overwhelming. Bob was nice enough, and cute in his way, but hard to imagine as a romantic partner. Imagining *herself* as a romantic partner was even more difficult.

Bob stared at the cardinal while Kaye continued to fret to herself. Intimacy was a tricky word. In some ways, the thought of being physically intimate with a man other than Stan was easier to fathom than sharing her innermost thoughts and feelings. She and Stan had been almost of one mind as their marriage lengthened. Their common experiences had morphed into a shorthand way of communicating. They finished each other's sentences and often punctuated the commentary with laughter and hugs. How would she ever duplicate that kind of connection with Bob, or any man? Did she want to? As Kristen would say, the "emotional work" would be difficult.

"I understand," Bob finally said, though he didn't seem to. "As I said, no offense intended. What were you saying about a dinner club?"

Kaye described her vague plan of having a monthly carry-in for their cul-de-sac. Not only would the members have a hearty meal, but the planning, shopping, and decorating would consume time and encourage fellowship.

"What about guys like me?" Bob asked. "I can't cook, except to defrost and microwave. What would I contribute?"

On a roll now, Kaye's eyes sparkled. "You could bring paper goods, obviously, and help with cleanup. Or you could enroll in the cooking classes Gordon Park has each week. Or you might tend to the grill during the summer months. There are lots of possibilities."

"Maybe it's worth considering," Bob admitted. He checked his phone and added, "But for now, I've got to get home. I feel the need for a snack, and my glucose monitor agrees with me."

Kaye was concerned, but she knew Bob's pride had taken a blow today. "Then let's get you home," she said. *And I'll be checking out how safe you really are when we get there.*

Bob unlocked his front door and Kaye followed him in. This woman was determined to take care of him. All he wanted was a little fun and someone to flirt with. Which, according to his wife, had been his downfall at times since fun and flirtation had sometimes not involved her. Now Kaye was practically nursing him while she surveyed his living room with a caregiver's eye.

"Bob, you've got way too many throw rugs around," she said. "They're lovely, but very dangerous. Fall hazards, you know?"

"My kids have said the same thing," he grumbled. "But I like them. They remind me of the travels Barb and I took when she was alive."

"Then we'll turn them into wall hangings or pillows," Kaye said over her shoulder as she made her way into the kitchen.

She was actually checking his cabinets and refrigerator! "Kaye, what are you doing?" he asked. "Can't a man have a little privacy?"

"I'm getting a sense of how you live," she replied. "Bob, you've said your diabetes requires regular, nutritious meals and snacks. Other than the frozen dinners, you don't have much here." She frowned and said, "Your produce crisper is empty! Canned green beans are not going to help you."

Bob slumped into a chair. "As I said, I need a snack. Hand me one of the apples in that bowl, please?"

Kaye obliged, but not before slicing it and adding a little peanut butter to each piece. For a second he hoped she'd finished her tirade about his poor eating habits. No such luck.

"I've got it! You and I are going to the grocery store together this week, Bob. I'm due for my regular trip and based on what I see here, so are you. I'll introduce you to lots of foods that are easy to prepare and good for you. What do you say?"

"Okay," Bob said weakly, between bites of apple. "I don't have a choice, do I?"

"No, you really don't," Kaye said. "I've got to be going, but I'll call you tomorrow about our shopping trip." She turned to leave, then planted a gentle kiss on Bob's cheek. "Talk soon."

Well, I wanted romance. But this woman was more of a nurse's aide than lover. A peck on the cheek was more motherly than passionate. Maybe he should give Linda a call.

Kaye spent the rest of her day cleaning her already clean home and making a grocery list for tomorrow. If she didn't snag Bob soon, he'd figure out an assortment of excuses to avoid the grocery trip. She was ready for a Netflix binge when her phone rang.

"Kristen, how are you?" she asked. "How's that darling baby of yours?"

"She's fine, Mom," Kristen answered. "Still chubby and full of spunk. What have you been up to?"

Kristen always seemed to sense when Kaye had something new in the works. Kaye had planned to tell her about Bob but not this soon. Remembering her vow to be honest, she said, "Well, I've been walking faithfully, despite the chilly weather. Our group has lost motivation." She paused, then added, "Except for me and Bob, that is. We're regular walkers."

"Bob Benson? That Bob?"

"Yes, honey. That Bob. We're becoming friends. I know that may be hard for you. Tell me what you think."

"I think it's good, Mom. I've told you he made amends and that I've forgiven him. But what do you mean by *friends?*"

"Just that. Friends who help each other and share how things are going. He's having some health issues and eats terribly. We're going to the market together tomorrow and I'll guide his purchases a bit."

Kristen laughed. "Mom, I was wondering how long it would take for your caregiver personality to manifest at Gordon Park. Katie and I even had a bet. I won, now that I know you're in full mothering mode. Katie thought it would take you another month."

Unsure if she was annoyed or amused by her girls and their financial interest in her choices, Kaye just chuckled. "Speaking of Katie, how do you think she'll react to my friendship with Bob? She can be a little tougher than you."

"You're right. I'd tell her before she hears from someone else. Katie was always angrier at Bob than I was. She couldn't believe his grief colored his behavior so much that he was inappropriate with you. Her experience with the church in Phoenix has hardened her a bit."

"I agree," Kaye said. "I pray for you both, of course, but I worry about Katie. There's an edge to her that didn't used to be there. I'll call her after we talk."

They spent the next fifteen minutes catching up on Kristen, Mike, Michelle, and Sophie. While Kristen's life wasn't perfect *(whose was?)* Kaye was confident that her older daughter's path was smooth for now. Time to call Katie.

Katie answered on the first ring. Kaye knew she was eating supper in front of the television. "Katie, I was about to binge the latest romantic comedy. What are you watching?"

"Nothing that insipid," her daughter muttered. Catching herself, she backtracked. "Sorry, Mom. I'm looking for a good murder mystery. Lovebird stuff isn't my choice these days."

"I understand," Kaye said. "Can you put your mystery on pause for a few minutes? I want to run something by you."

"Sure, Mom. Are you okay? Do you need my help?"

Kaye marveled at the similarities between herself and her younger daughter. Helpers to the end, no matter how miserable their own lives might be. Well, Katie would have something other than her own troubles to think about after Kaye told her about Bob.

"No, I don't need your help, Katie. I just wanted you to know I've developed a friendship with a man who lives nearby. Nothing serious, but we walk together most mornings and we're going to start a supper club here at Gordon Park."

Kaye heard Katie sniff. Her girl knew there was more to the story. "Nothing serious. I get it, Mom. So why tell me? Why call late in the evening?" Pausing a beat, Katie circled in. "Obviously, I'm going to balk at the man you're discussing. Who is it?"

"Bob Benson," Kaye replied. "He worked at GCC before you were on staff." Kaye cringed at her own cowardice. She should have just reminded Katie of Bob's history with Kristen.

"The power-hungry, perverted Bob Benson?" Katie shrieked. "The man who almost ruined Kristen's chance for tenure after hitting on a new widow who happened to be her mother? Mom, you can't be serious."

"I'm serious, Katie. He's a flawed man, but then

we all have our issues. Kristen, by the way, is fine with my friendship. She's accepted his apologies and understands the pain he was in after his wife died."

"Sweet," Katie said sarcastically. "Too bad he didn't have a clue about *your* pain after Dad died."

"He's also apologized to me. And I've accepted his remorse and regret. Anyway, I'll choose my own friends, but I wanted you to know about him. He's not a healthy man. I'm helping him with good nutrition and so forth." Kaye knew her explanation was weak. Katie was like a bloodhound when it came to her mother's hedging.

"As always, you're the world's best helper, Mom. I think it's more than friendship between you and Bob, so I'll just say this. Be careful. Don't get sucked in so much that helping hurts you in the long run." After a few seconds, Katie had the grace to add, "Like I did."

Kaye sent a prayer of thanks that the call ended on a fairly positive note. As she searched for a light movie, her phone rang. Thinking it was Katie again, she answered, "What now, honey? I thought we'd ended our talk."

"Honey? Thanks for that, Kaye. I was feeling like an invalid geriatric patient after you left today." Bob laughed into the phone, more lighthearted than he'd been a few hours ago.

Flustered, Kaye sputtered, "Bob? I thought it was Katie. Are you all right?"

Irritated, Bob said, "There you go. Back in caregiver mode. I'm fine, Kaye. Believe it or not, I was checking the grocery ads online. The specials start tomorrow. Should we hit the market in the morning?"

"Great minds," Kaye chortled. "Want to pick me up at ten?"

"Sure, it's a date," Bob said. "Or not a date. Whatever you want to call it."

The Gordon Kroger wasn't busy at this time of morning, which Kaye had counted on. If she was going to instruct Bob on the finer points of grocery shopping, they needed a quiet atmosphere and empty aisles. Scanning Bob's pathetic list, she tried to be diplomatic.

"I see you plan to replace your frozen dinners, Bob. Let's also try to buy a few add-ons to make them more like real meals." Steering her cart to the produce section, Bob was forced to follow.

"I'm not a big vegetable fan," he whined. "Barb made salads and mashed potatoes. Occasionally we'd have canned corn."

"Sure, those are good," Kaye said with a smile. "But let's try at least one new thing a few times next week." Kaye pointed to the stoplight packages of bell peppers, their vivid colors practically begging to be bought, and asked, "What about adding a bell pepper to your salads? And maybe some diced carrots? You'd have a dandy salad in no time."

"Do they sell this stuff already cut up?" Bob asked. "I'm not good with a knife, and when I'm hungry, I'm hungry. I don't have time for all this prep if my sugar is low."

"That's the second step of good nutrition," Kaye said, a little smugly. "Buying your food is the first, then prepping in advance is the second. You can make up a whole bag of salad, enough to last several days, when we get home. Easy as pie."

"Pie," Bob whined again. "I'd kill for pie."

Kaye giggled and turned to get a package of peppers. Suddenly, she was facing Rose Dolce. "Oh, hi, Rose. I see you're an early shopper like me. How are you?"

"I'm well," Rose said. "Hello, Mr. Benson." Making no attempt to be subtle, she asked, "Are you two here with each other? I didn't know you were friendly enough to go Krogering together."

Kaye couldn't contain herself. She held her belly and laughed out loud. "Krogering? My goodness, Rose. You make it sound almost dirty."

Rose snorted and waved them away as she directed her cart to the bakery. "On my way. I'll call you this afternoon, Kaye." Looking at Bob, she added, "I'm headed to the bakery, Bob. They have a special on their Dutch apple crumb pies. Just so you know."

Kaye finished her lunch and marveled that Bob hadn't known how to make a simple tuna salad sandwich. Good thing she had instructed him, leaving him with two days' worth of fresh lunches. Bob purchased sliced carrot and celery sticks, along with bags of varietal lettuce. One thing at a time, she told herself. No sense in burning Bob out with too many changes to his diet.

She was cleaning her kitchen after putting the groceries away when her phone rang with its generic ringtone. Rose Dolce got right to the point.

"Kaye, what did I tell you? I'll bet you've already progressed from 'friend' to surrogate housekeeper and cook. This is a path to disaster, believe me. Bob Benson will use you blind, and then drop you for a younger gal when he's feeling better. He's a womanizer, don't you remember, Kaye? He was all over you when you were a vulnerable widow."

"Hello to you, too, Rose," Kaye said. "It's always a pleasure to be on the receiving end of your lectures. It makes me feel young, about twelve years old in fact."

"No need to get huffy," Rose said. "I'm simply pointing out what everyone in Gordon knows. Bob Benson is trouble. Trouble in the worst way, because he's needy. He'll use you blind, wait and see."

"You're repeating yourself, Rose," Kaye replied. "Consider me warned and let it go. We've been friends for ages, watched our girls grow into fine women, and I don't want to end our relationship. But you have to admit if I treated you the way you're talking to me, you'd be mad."

Silence greeted Kaye. She was ready to end the call when Rose said, "Fine. I get it, Kaye. I'll back off. But I love you and want the best for you." With that, Rose hung up.

She always has to have the last word, Kaye thought. And she always ends things feeling martyred for her good intentions. But Rose would get over it, and the next time they ran into each other, they would be friends again. Kaye suddenly remembered why she'd left Gordon. Sometimes having everyone know your business was downright smothering.

Chapter Nine

Laughing at the students' banter down the hall from her office, Katie turned back to her computer monitor. Things seemed to be going well. With only a few exceptions, this semester's interns were working hard. Their faculty sponsors had helped Katie when she'd given the slackers her "get with the program" speech by also calling the students in for stern lectures. Her latest meeting with Dr. King had been positive. The campus gossip network had kept him informed about her improved dealings with Louis. Evidently, Dr. King had also met with Louis, who had been on equally good behavior. That was significant, she had to admit.

Fortunately, there had been no campus chatter about her last meeting with Louis at the diner. She'd left angry at his refusal to compromise, or at least listen to her new proposal for "culinary lite" internships, jobs in which his students could study the business or regulatory side of the restaurant industry instead of focusing solely on food preparation and service.

In Louis' defense, Katie admitted she'd stormed out of the meeting before she had explained her thoughts. Thank goodness she'd grabbed her salad. No diner had a right to make a Caesar salad that good. Which is what she would have forced Louis to admit had she stayed. But she'd left. When was her temper going to stay in check?

She'd been more controlled with her mother when Kaye had announced her "friendship" with Bob Benson. Katie knew better. Her mom would be dating Bob in a matter of weeks. But Louis brought out the worst in her. His smug attitude, his captivating eyes, and the *nerve* to take her hand in the middle of a professional discussion all signaled trouble. Why did people not recognize what a shifty character he was?

He had his strengths, she knew. He cared for GCC students, to the point of buying half a cow for his food lab. That was lovely, but when was he going to realize that these kids needed paying jobs, even if they weren't in Michelin-rated restaurants? She shook her head and focused back on the essays she had to grade before her career class met at three.

A knock on her office door derailed that plan. Kyle Montrose, a culinary arts second-year student, stood in the doorway. Kyle looked dejected. Katie had a bad feeling, knowing without asking the cause of his distress.

"Kyle, what's going on?" she asked. "Anything I can help with?"

"I'm not sure, Ms. Anderson," he answered, flopping down on the chair beside her desk. "I don't know what to do. Chef M is really pissed at me." Kyle reddened, and added, "I mean angry at me. Sorry."

"No problem, Kyle. Why is Chef M angry?"

"I've taken an early-commit job as a manager with a burger franchise. They made me a great offer, and I'll be able to work half-time next semester before I graduate. There are possible upper-level management slots for me in the future. Chef says I've sold out, that I'll never amount to anything in the gourmet world, and that I've wasted my years in college."

Kyle was near tears, obviously distraught that his idol had berated him so fiercely. "He wouldn't listen when I told him about my hefty school loans and about my nephew who lives with mom and me. I've got to help them out. My sister is MIA with her latest loser boyfriend, totally ignoring her kid. I've got to get my loans paid off as soon as I can."

Katie dug her fingernails into her palms. If Louis were in the room, she'd have slapped him silly. Whatever. She had Kyle in the room, not Louis. She channeled her inner Kristen and stayed cool.

"It sounds to me like you've made a considered decision, Kyle. A decision that will benefit you and your family. Your degree will still be useful when your loans and other bills are paid. There will always be chef jobs to be had." Katie knew she was spouting platitudes, but at least she was calm.

"I tried to tell Chef M all that!" Kyle shouted.

Students in the hall were looking into Katie's office. She rose and quietly closed the door. "I'm sure you did," she said. "Sounds like he didn't want to hear you, at least for now. Maybe Chef M will cool off in a little while."

Kyle studied Katie and shrugged. "You've dealt with him, Ms. Anderson. Do you think he'll cool off any time soon?"

That question served to cut the tension a bit. Katie laughed, and after a pause, so did Kyle. "So, what's your next step, Kyle? Here are your options, as I see them, though I'll bet you'll think of more. One, you could let Chef M cool off and come to you." Noting Kyle's skeptical look, she continued. "Two, you could ask someone to intervene on your behalf. Maybe Dr. King?"

"No, I don't want to bring in the bigwigs," Kyle said. "Could you talk to him?"

She knew she wasn't a "bigwig," but it stung to hear it said out loud. Katie smiled. "You've probably noticed I don't have a lot of pull with Chef M. I doubt I'd help your case."

Suddenly Kyle looked like a sage. "Oh, you'd be surprised, Ms. Anderson. Chef M looks at you like my girlfriend looks at me."

This time, Katie didn't laugh or smile. "Kyle, you must be feverish. Believe me, Chef M barely tolerates me on the same elevator. But we'll figure this out." Katie glanced at the clock and said, "I've got to run to make my class. Stay positive and stop by at the end of the week."

After class and meeting individually with students unclear about the latest assignment, Katie reflected on her conversation with Kyle. He was carrying heavy burdens for a guy barely in his twenties. Why couldn't Louis get that? Junior chefs made minimum wage at best, with the attraction of free meals a minimal benefit. Kids like Kyle needed more than the daily kitchen freebie. They needed hard cash, and they needed it now.

Katie sighed, and noticed for the second time

today that the leaves on the trees outside her office were starting to turn color. Academia had holiday breaks going for it, she mused. Soon she'd be eating her mom's moist turkey, sausage stuffing, and pumpkin cheesecake, with three more days off to begin her holiday shopping. The insurance industry was not helpful around the holidays, since that's when many people had accidents.

Recalling her old job still stung. Katie had tried to wait out all the gossip, all the ugly talk about her and her divorcing coworker. The office atmosphere had finally quieted down, but surprise of all surprises, her church acquaintances became more and more condemning. She had actually been called into the office of the junior pastor to explain her involvement in the divorce that had everyone talking. To this day, he didn't believe her explanation about helping a friend through a devastating loss.

She packed her laptop and was grateful for the quiet night at home ahead. Katie forced herself to remember that most people were good, that most good intentions were not punished, and that she had many things to be thankful for. She had almost convinced herself when she saw Louis standing outside her office. Sending up a quick prayer, she stayed calm.

"Louis, I'm on my way out. Hopefully, what you need can wait until tomorrow."

"It won't take long," Louis said. "I wanted to warn you that Kyle Montrose might want to talk to you."

"Why would I need a warning?" Katie studied Louis' confident posture, his casual slouch against her office door frame. What a poser. "Kyle is a good kid, no warning needed."

"Oh, you'll see," Louis said, seeming a bit discomfited. "Kyle wants my blessing on a job he's taken. It's a total waste of his training and talent. Of course, I refused to give it to him. He left my office without listening to me."

Katie wanted to shout her response, but again, God was helping her stay calm. "Whatever he wants with me, Louis, it's no business of yours. Sounds like you gave him your input. I've got nothing to do with that, right? You're the culinary artist, not me."

Louis looked confused. "So, did Kyle talk to you or not? What's your take on his situation?"

"I've got to run, Louis. As I indicated, I don't disclose confidential student matters with faculty, unless they've given me permission." Never mind that Kyle had asked her to talk to Louis. She didn't want to just yet.

"I'm sure he's got you all sympathetic about his family dilemma," Louis groaned. "It's nothing he can't work out while still taking a job befitting his skills. Surely you understand, Katie."

Katie lugged her tote bag over her shoulder and hooked her lunch satchel at her elbow as she locked her door. "Good night, Louis," she said. "I've got to run."

What would Kristen call her approach with Louis? Passive-aggressive, maybe? Katie didn't care. Instead, she labeled her dismissive style as a power play with a man overcome with ego. She'd let Louis stew (*Ha—food pun!*) tonight, then she'd call him first thing in the morning to discuss Kyle.

It was a good plan, but Louis hadn't been informed. He dogged her footsteps to her car, talking nonstop, ending with, "Believe me, Katie, I want what's best for Kyle."

"Me, too," she responded with a fake smile. "Have a good evening, Louis." She had her car in gear before Louis could answer. For once, the GCC lot was clear and she made a speedy turn onto the main road bordering campus.

A quick stop at the grocery yielded all of Katie's comfort foods. In honor of the Thanksgiving holiday only eight days away, she bought a frozen microwavable turkey dinner. Kyle's words came back to her. According to Kyle, Louis had taunted him with the use of frozen foods by the chain that was to be Kyle's employer. *Who doesn't use frozen foods?* Katie wondered. She had a full chest freezer in her garage that saved the day countless times when her bank account was low. And she'd learned from Kaye to buy two frozen turkeys each year when they were loss leaders around the holidays. Louis knew nothing.

Louis trudged into his home, throwing his jacket in the direction of the sofa. Normally neat, he figured he had all night to hang the stupid thing up. He meandered to the kitchen and grabbed a beer from the fridge. Taking a big first gulp, he thought of Katie's refusal to talk about Kyle. What had Katie meant when she said she wanted what was best for Kyle? Surely, she would understand the waste of the young man's gifts at the chain specializing in burgers named for each day of the week. Money would come, if Kyle had the patience to wait for it. Yes, his family needed his extra income, but they needed to see the big picture. Maybe Louis would talk to Kyle's mom.

Or not. He remembered something about confidentiality rules with college students, and Kyle was over twenty-one. Louis could get in big trouble if he interfered in a family matter. He missed his work in Europe, where he was the ultimate boss. His word was law in his restaurants.

Of course, being the big boss had its drawbacks, especially when the economy turned sour and people couldn't afford weekly gourmet outings. He sat down hard on the sofa, splashing beer on the cushion. It all came back to him like a boulder on his chest.

That terrible feeling, that sense that your world was about to crumble if the bills didn't get paid. He recalled begging his creditors for extra time on his accounts, receiving it the majority of the time. He remembered his parents' concern when they knew he was struggling without knowing the reason. Then his father got sick and they focused on that. Louis' concerns were more easily hidden then they talked about his father's treatment.

Even worse was Marie-Christine's pity. No, not even pity, but a mixture of condescension and disdain. Suddenly the hot chef was not a suitable partner for the British duchess. She became very busy with her charity projects and found new "walkers" to escort her to events. Louis knew he was out of her life when one of his cooks showed him a photo from *Hello* magazine. Marie-Christine was gazing at a man who looked a lot like Louis. His cook made a joke about the duchess trying to replace him. Louis knew it wasn't a joke.

Then Louis had his epiphany, sloshing more beer

on the couch. Kyle was in the same spot of trouble, only the health and well-being of his family was at stake. How could he have missed that? When Louis was broke, he was able to get by until business picked up. His dad had been sick, but his parents had each other and the resources to handle his father's treatment. Kyle didn't have that luxury. His mother and nephew needed him desperately.

Louis texted Katie that he was on his way over to her place. He turned his phone off so that her reply would be undeliverable. No sense in letting her say no.

Thanking God that Gordon was such a small town, Louis was banging on Katie's door within ten minutes. She answered in a fury, opening the door so hard it hit the wall behind it. Again, he liked this side of her. Katie was very attractive when her eyes were flashing, and her cheeks were flushed.

"I'm in no mood, Louis," she said. "I texted you not to come, but it either didn't go through or you're stalking me."

"Weird. Technology glitches happen a lot, don't they?" Louis asked. "This won't take long. May I come in?"

Katie opened the door wide enough for him to pass. She didn't ask him to sit or offer a drink. Standing with her arms crossed over her chest, she said, "You're on the clock, Louis. Talk fast."

"I've come to realize I misjudged the situation with Kyle. You've probably already told him the chain job is fine, given his family demands and school loans. You're right."

Katie was dumbfounded. And deflated. He grinned at her lack of righteous anger.

"What caused this change of heart?" she asked.

"Maybe God gave me a shake," Louis said, pointing to the ceiling. "I needed to be reminded of a time in my life when I scrambled for money, when others were depending on me and I felt powerless to help."

Katie arched her brows, which Louis also liked. She was a challenge. "Okay, I'll listen," she said. "Have a seat."

Still no offer of a beverage, he thought. But at least he was sitting, and Katie was listening.

"My restaurants in Europe went through a bad patch during the last downturn of the economy. My dad got sick at the same time. I found out who my true friends were, and I learned I could economize in ways I still shudder at today." He scrubbed his eyes and continued. "I came through it all and paid my bills. My parents had the money for Dad's chemo and radiation. I was in a lot better shape than Kyle and his family, but I know that terrible feeling. That knot in your stomach and pressure on your chest that keeps you up at night with worry and dread. I guess I finally have some empathy for Kyle."

"It's about time," Katie said. "Good for you. Do you want to tell Kyle tomorrow? I'd strongly recommend it. He idolizes you for some mysterious reason and is grieving at your disapproval."

Louis gazed at Katie. She was still angry but cooling a bit. He smiled at her.

"Don't you be smiling that dreamy smile at me, Louis Masson," she snarled. "I'm not some college kid who can be manipulated by your charms." She smoothed the throw pillow on her lap and sipped her iced tea. "You finally understand what Kyle is going through. Maybe with time you'll have empathy for your other students."

"I will, I'm sure," Louis said. "But let's talk more about my dreamy smile."

Rolling her eyes, Katie stayed firm. "You know your smile is a real 'come hither' look," she said. "The girls in the hall outside my office talk about it at least once a day. But they don't know you like I do."

Louis crossed the room and sat next to Katie on the wing chair meant for one person. "No, they don't know me like you do," he said. "Let's get to know each other even better."

He kissed her. She didn't fight him, and in fact she kissed him back. After a long twenty seconds, they broke away, each short of breath. "Isn't it fun to get to know each other?" he whispered.

Katie leaped out of the chair, a difficult task since they were wedged in together, and said, "You need to leave, Louis. I'm expecting my mom any minute."

"Weak excuse, Katie. I'll leave if you want but I know your mom isn't coming over."

At that point the doorbell rang, and Kaye Anderson let herself in. "Katie, it's me. What have I told you about not keeping your door locked? You're asking for trouble."

Katie looked triumphant and pointed Louis to the door. He saluted her and greeted Kaye. "Hello, Mrs. Anderson. Katie and I had some unfinished business with a student. You two have a nice visit."

As he walked across the tiny porch, Louis heard Kaye say, "Katie, he's a real hunk! Are you two an item?"

Louis laughed all the way to his car. Despite the fantastic kiss, he was also concerned. Was Katie still angry? Could they be an item? As he opened the driver's side door, he realized he wanted to be an item with Katie. Her passion, integrity, and that appealing sultry look combined to almost bewitch him. What in God's name had he ever seen in the duchess?

"Come on, tell me, Katie," Kaye insisted. "What's going on with you and that man? He's a doll."

Katie pressed her temple. She was sure a migraine was coming on. Louis had done an absolute about-face. He agreed with her about Kyle's situation. He said she'd been right all along. But then he'd kissed her. What a kiss! Thank goodness her mother had dropped by, serving to end what seemed like a potentially passionate time on the wing chair and accidently endorsing Katie's lie that Kaye was on her way.

"I don't know, Mom," she said weakly. "He gives me nothing but grief at work, but he's also smart and loves his students. I'll admit he's a looker." Katie looked at Kaye with watery eyes.

"Remember when I said Dan and I were too much alike, each of us wanting to plot our future with no surprises? I wanted more passion, more whimsy out of life. I think God is teasing me by putting Louis Masson at GCC. He's full of all those things and more. What a mess."

"Doesn't sound like a mess to me," Kaye said. "Sounds like fun, if you let it happen. What's holding you back from getting to know Louis better?"

"We're coworkers on a small campus, Mom! If it goes badly, I'll have to see him almost daily. As I said, it's a mess."

"You're making your own mess, honey. When I told you I was friends with Bob, you were honest with me, even though we didn't agree. I'm going to offer you the same courtesy." Kaye settled into the armchair and sipped the bottled water she'd helped herself to. "You can't avoid men forever, Katie. Be done with Dan and let it go. And be done with the guy you nurtured through his divorce."

Katie bristled. "I was just being a friend," she said, standing up from the wing chair. "Everyone took it the wrong way."

"Perhaps," Kaye said. "My hunch is that you liked that man, about whom you've never confided in me. I don't even know his name. That's odd, don't you think?"

Katie walked to the sofa and sat down with a plop. Her mother was half psychic, she was sure. "*Perhaps* you're right, Mom. His name was Glenn. I liked him well enough. As he went through the pain of his divorce, and the financial agony of his settlement, I guess I thought we'd be a good team." Katie studied her nails, turned to her mother and said, "Okay, you're correct. I was disappointed that Glenn didn't return my feelings. I'm pretty needy, huh?"

"No, you aren't needy. You just need to meet the right man."

"But Louis can't be the right man, Mom. He just can't."

"He could be if you'd let him in," Kaye said. "I love you Katie. I only want what's best for you, just as you do for me. And we're both grown women, more than able to make good choices. I trust that you'll do that by giving Louis a chance. And you've got to trust me by letting me figure out what's going on with me and Bob."

Katie laughed. "Nice job working Bob into the conversation, Mom. You're right, yet again. We're both smart women, capable of running our own lives."

After a pause, Katie asked, "Why did you come over, Mom? Is something wrong?"

Kaye laughed so hard she snorted. "I was coming to give you a lecture about letting me live my own life. Turns out you and Louis made it easy!"

Chapter Ten

Thanksgiving had come and gone. It had been a good holiday weekend, Katie thought, as she sat through a never-ending committee report during the faculty/staff meeting. Her mother had outdone herself cooking all the traditional foods in her new kitchen, though she had invited Bob Benson over for the meal. Since Kristen and her family were friendly to him, Katie had no choice but to be cordial as well. He seemed nice enough, but as Katie knew, that could mean nothing.

A request from the faculty/staff chair for a roll call vote yanked her back into the present. After that, the meeting plodded on as usual. There were the typical turf wars between departments, each small unit juggling ways to attract more students and ensure the survival of liberal arts majors. Katie thought it was a shame the majors were vulnerable; she had a business background but had loved her sociology and psychology courses. What would the world be like if numbers and formulas were the only things that mattered?

She was thinking about her next day's schedule when she heard her name mentioned as one of the new staff members specially invited to participate in the Christmas cookie contest. Proceeds would benefit the GCC food pantry. She glanced at her sister. Kristen shook her head and silently mouthed, "You don't have to do it." Katie smiled but was secretly annoyed. Kristen knew she wasn't a cook, much less a baker. But why did she have to remind Katie publicly of that fact?

Katie looked up and saw Louis preening. He was already sure of his victory. As the social committee chair droned on about the categories involved (gourmet, easy, kid-friendly, and innovative), Louis looked more and more confident. Katie rolled her eyes at his assurance. He probably thought he'd win each category! Suddenly, she was motivated to learn to bake.

Not that she would win any awards, but she could certainly participate. She wouldn't be at Louis' level, but it would be a good way to meet other faculty members, therefore increasing her chances of filling internship spots going forward. And there was an "easy" category! God was telling her to enter, right? She'd ask her mother for some recipes.

After the meeting, Kristen called out. "Katie, do you have a minute?"

Surprised at Kristen's tense look, Katie said, "Sure, Sis. Are you okay?"

"I'm good, but I need a favor."

Kristen didn't look good. She looked edgy and a little sad, which was out of character for her. Katie squeezed her big sister's hand and said, "How can I help?"

"Mike and I need a sitter for Friday night," Kristen said. "Mom is busy with Bob and my regular sitter is going to the big Gordon High School football game." She paused and looked directly at Katie. "Mike and I really need a night out. Michelle is teething yet again, and Sophie is a little difficult lately. So, you have the big picture. Are you game?"

Struck by Kristen's obvious tension, Katie decided to make her sister a better offer. "Let's up the ante, Kris. Why don't the girls stay over at my place Friday night? We could have a slumber party. Does Michelle still sleep well in her packable bed?"

Kristen stopped the flow of bodies leaving the meeting and hugged Katie. "Thanks a lot, Katie. That would be wonderful. Sophie likes you and will be thrilled to stay at any house that's not mine. And Michelle will sleep anywhere as long as she has her stuffed dinosaur and a chilled teething ring."

"Then it's a date," Katie said, a little too loudly. "Bring the girls by around seven on Friday evening. And have fun."

Kristen hustled off to pick up Michelle at daycare. Katie walked to her car alone but was stopped by Louis before she could unlock her door.

"You have a date?" he asked. "Is your sister fixing you up with someone?"

"None of your business, Louis. Let's talk about that cookie contest. Are you going to enter?" Katie knew this would irritate him. She was right.

"You bet I'm entering!" Louis said. "How can the director of the culinary arts program not enter in all categories? What an absurd question!"

"Me too," Katie said with a grin. "Maybe not all categories, but a couple. It will be fun."

Louis looked injured. "Once again, you don't take my profession seriously, Katie. Christmas cookies should be art forms, not fun." "You've got a lot to learn about Christmas cookies. And maybe about Christmas itself. Lighten up, Louis."

"I'll lighten up if you tell me about your date when we get back to school on Monday," he answered.

"I'd be happy to," Katie said, as she swung into the driver's seat. "Take care, Louis."

Katie laughed to herself as she turned out of the campus main drive. Louis actually sounded jealous. But that wasn't possible.

Kaye stared at her phone in wonder. Katie had called, asking to come over and go through Christmas cookie recipes. She loved her youngest daughter, but the girl was not a cook. This would be interesting.

Katie arrived, straight from campus evidently. She was still wearing her casual work outfit, a cute pair of slim slacks and a boat-neck sweater with a strappy camisole peeking out at the shoulder. Kaye was surprised. Katie usually wore what Kaye referred to as "buttoned-up" outfits, meaning minimal skin and offering no hint of her body shape. Despite her protests about the man, Kaye knew Katie was unconsciously dressing for Louis.

"Christmas cookies, huh?" Kaye asked as she helped Katie with her coat. "What gives?"

"There's a contest at work. It's a good way for me to network with faculty members." Katie plopped down on the nearest bar stool at Kaye's kitchen island. "But as you know, I'm no baker. Will you help me, Mom?" Katie batted her eyes and smiled.

Kaye laughed. Katie could be a little brittle, but she was funny when she needed to be. Nonetheless, Kaye teased back. "I'd love to help. What are you and Louis going to make as your entry?"

Katie didn't take the bait. "Funny, Mom. Louis will probably make some over-the-top French concoction that's too beautiful for anyone to enjoy. I just need an easy recipe. And maybe one suitable for the kid's category."

They spent the next hour looking through Kaye's recipe box, in between Katie's barbs about the value of putting the recipes in digital form. The vast collection of cookbooks was also studied. After commenting on the sorry state of some of Kaye's tattered and soiled books, Katie finally decided on a couple of recipe options. Kaye ignored her teasing about the cookbooks, noting that they were well-used and well-loved.

"Thanks, Mom. I'll get to the store and buy the ingredients for these two and start to practice." She looked pleased with herself, then snapped her fingers. "I've got it! I'll have Sophie help me when she stays over on Friday night."

"You could ask," Kaye said. "But maybe Sophie will want to chill and watch movies."

Katie studied her mother. "Why would you say that? Sophie will be fine."

"I'm sure she will be." Kaye debated saying more and decided Katie needed more background. "Have you noticed your sister has been a little frazzled lately?"

"Actually, I have. What's wrong?"

"This is all in confidence, Katie. But Sophie has been difficult recently. Kristen is suddenly the evil stepmother. It's hard on her. And raising a toddler is hard too. Mike is a fine husband and father, but the load falls on Kristen due to his job at the hospital." Kaye paused and figured she might as well be honest. "Kristen called me crying a few nights ago. She's overwhelmed with Sophie's attitude. Sophie's latest demand is for a cell phone, which she insists all of her friends have. She just turned eleven!"

"I'm sorry to hear this, Mom. It explains a lot. Thanks for telling me. What does Mike say about the cell phone?"

"He's not much help," Kaye admitted. "Given the scary events in schools, he's all for Sophie being able to call him or Kristen if she needs to. But Kristen is concerned about social media, online predators, and all that."

Katie looked at her mother. After a beat, she said, "What you're leaving unsaid is that this isn't that big a deal. Most kids are getting phones earlier and earlier. Parental controls help to keep danger away. What I'm wondering is if Kristen feels unsupported by Mike. In areas other than just Sophie. Am I right?"

"You nailed it, Katie. Kristen isn't too happy with Mike at the moment. That's why they need time alone. I must confess that I'm the one who suggested Kristen call you to babysit. She needs her sister."

"And because you're busy with Bob," Katie sneered. "Right?"

"Yes. I have plans with Bob. If you think you

need help with Sophie and Michelle, I'll ask him to reschedule."

"No, I'm good. Thanks again for filling me in, Mom. But don't turn your phone off Friday night. Just in case I need help!"

"It's a deal. Good luck, honey. You're a good sister."

Friday evening at seven, Kristen dropped off Michelle and all her toddler gear while Sophie dawdled in the back seat of the car. "Come on, Soph! I need to pick up your dad at the hospital."

Sophie trudged through Katie's front lawn, deliberately stepping into the leaf piles Katie had raked earlier in the week. Kristen shrugged and wished Katie good luck.

Michelle was content to watch the latest episode of some animated doggie show, for which Katie was grateful. She tried to engage Sophie as they unloaded the groceries for making cookies.

"What's new with you, Soph?" Katie asked. "And thanks in advance for helping me

with the cookies. You may have heard I'm no whiz in the kitchen."

Sophie grinned. "I've heard you're *terrible,* Aunt Katie. Dad still talks about the way you burned the sweet potatoes one year at Christmas. And Kristen told me about the time you toasted a batch of meatballs by using the centigrade temperature on the food thermometer."

"So sweet of you to remind me," Katie shot back, knowing she had to hold her ground with the touchy preteen. They both laughed. Katie decided to take a risk. "What's going on with you at school? What are the new trends for sixth graders?"

"Well, cell phones are trending. Not that I'd know about that. Kristen is ridiculous. She's always so worried about things." Sophie took a big bite of the chocolate chip bakery cookie Katie had purchased. "According to your sister, I'll be sold into a sex-trafficking ring or be bullied until I can't take it. She's so old!"

Katie knew Sophie was exaggerating. As Kaye had said, Kristen was being cast as the bad guy while Mike worked his long hours. Sophie's transparent tactic was to lay on the drama with her aunt in hopes she would intervene with Kristen. Nope, that wasn't going to happen.

"She loves you, Sophie. I'm not going to apologize for my sister for that." Katie paused. "I'm not sure if I should tell you this, but I've got some experience with online bullying."

Eyes wide, Sophie asked, "What do you mean? Were you a bully?"

Whoa. This kid was not nearly as loveable as she had been a few years ago. Katie let it slide. "No, I wasn't a bully. I was bullied."

"I doubt it," Sophie said. "You're a grown-up. Even if people were a little mean, you can handle that stuff."

"Oh, I handled it all right. I needed to get counseling and then I joined a support group."

Sophie's veneer of haughtiness disappeared. "I'm sorry, Aunt Katie. What happened?"

"This is all in confidence, girl. Understand?"

Sophie nodded. Katie debated the wisdom of

sharing it all, but Kristen needed her help. And whether Sophie ended up with a phone or not, she needed a reality check.

"A guy in my church in Phoenix was going through a bad divorce."

Sophie nodded again. "Yeah, my parents were mean to each other for a while when they split up. But I was too little to really get it."

"But you went through a tough time, didn't you, Soph? Anyway, this guy I worked with, Glenn, needed a lot of support. I was his best friend for several months while his wife's lawyer took him to the cleaners, both in terms of money and emotions. I was actually worried about him doing something rash for a while. But he got through it."

"Okay. What does bullying have to do with this?"

"After someone at my church got wind of our friendship, the parish turned out to be a hotbed of gossip. My connection with Glenn suddenly became the reason for his divorce, which was totally false. The final papers were drawn up weeks before I became Glenn's friend."

"What kind of gossip?" Sophie breathed.

Editing out the uglier comments she'd been subjected to, Katie said, "You can guess. I was a home-wrecker, a false Christian, and a needy woman." Katie swallowed hard and turned her head as she got the sheet pans out of her cupboard. "It hurt. But since it was all on social media, I couldn't even confront the people who were calling me such ugly names. I was powerless."

"You could have talked to the pastor," Sophie said. "He'd have helped."

"If the pastor had been like Reverend Taylor, you'd be right. But unfortunately, he wasn't. There were times I wondered if he was actually feeding the lies to other members. I learned a lot about people, but none of it was good."

Sophie jumped off the stool and hugged Katie. "Thanks for telling me. I won't say a word to anyone."

"Grandma knows, and so does Kristen. But other than that, keep a lid on it, okay?"

The rest of the evening was easy and pleasant. Michelle seemed to pick up on the relaxed atmosphere and went down for the count at seven-thirty. Katie and Sophie watched Christmas movies, since it was after Thanksgiving and therefore permitted by the mysterious cinema-viewing police.

Kristen arrived at ten on Saturday, anxious as she put Michelle into her car seat while Sophie gathered her things. "How was she?" Kristen asked.

"Michelle is a doll," Katie said. "She may be the sweetest baby ever." Katie kissed her niece and then said, "Sophie was also fine. We had a good talk. I shared a bit about my experience with online haters. It gave her a lot to think about. If you and Mike do allow her to get a phone, maybe my story will help her be a little cautious. Fingers crossed."

Kristen hugged Katie. "Mike and I had a good talk about the phone. We'll figure it out. Sounds like it will be easier thanks to you."

After the Sutliffs left, Katie straightened her house but didn't have the energy to clean the myriad of crumbs on the tables, sofa, and carpet. How did a toddler manage to insert crumbs under the glass-topped coffee table where the metal met the glass? Who knew? It was time to make cookies. Last night's efforts were best forgotten. She was almost as messy as Michelle. Her kitchen was a testament to that.

After two batches of wedding cake balls (one rock-hard and burned, and one soggy and under-baked), she gave up. Time for a nap. That's what weekends were for, right?

Kaye reflected on her previous evening with Bob. She was surprised at how much fun they'd had. Bob was funny but gentle as he recounted memories of his life with his wife. They'd had a good marriage, which Kaye was happy to hear. She'd talked about her life with Stan, raising the girls, and then dealing with his cancer. She was surprised at herself; she didn't get tearful or morose. Stan was gone, she would always love him, but life moved on. This was a good grief day—some were not.

Bob had complimented her cooking, as well he should have, and she praised his recent weight loss and improved blood sugars.

"It's not been easy," Bob said. "My life is much emptier without beer and chips when I watch football. But the increased exercise is how I met you, so I guess it's all been worth it."

Life was unpredictable. Who would have guessed she'd be dating her daughter's former nemesis? Her return to Indiana was another surprise. She'd been so sure that achingly cold winters were behind her. And the ultimate shock was that she was a home-owner again after years of living in an apartment in

Phoenix. She paraphrased the old Jewish quote and mused, "Man plans, and God laughs."

Kaye decided to tidy up the kitchen before going to the big-box store for cookie-making supplies. Katie had insisted she was ready for the baking lesson, complete with all the supplies needed, but Kaye knew better. Inevitably, there would be a crucial ingredient or piece of equipment missing, usually at a time in preparation requiring speed.

Once at the store, Kaye spent a leisurely hour going up each houseware aisle. She usually didn't allow herself this luxury, since she'd spend more money than she'd planned. As she perused bakeware, wondering if Katie had a large cookie sheet, a voice called out.

"Kaye Anderson, long time no see," Rose Dolce sang. "I thought you were avoiding me after our last talk."

Kaye smiled, determined to be kind but firm. "The phone works both ways, friend. How have you been?"

Rose launched into a lengthy account of her children's lives and her husband's successful hip replacement. "But we are blessed, aren't we, Kaye? We have our health, our loved ones, and we can enjoy life with few worries."

"Wise words, Rose," Kaye answered. "Tell Annie my girls say hello." Kaye turned to study cake decorating bags and tips, but Rose wasn't finished.

"How are you and Bob Benson doing? I hope you've cooled things off with him." Kindness almost took flight. Kaye smiled again, this time with more difficulty. "Why would I want to cool things off with Bob? He's a good person and an excellent neighbor. Rose, you're becoming very judgmental in your old age." Okay, she wasn't being too kind after all.

Rose smiled this time, relishing Kaye's discomfort. "Ah. You've not cooled things off at all. Sounds like they're heating up to me." She arranged the items in her cart (mostly processed foods, Kaye observed to herself) and went on. "Mark my words, Kaye. That sugar diabetes is nothing to sneeze at. Bob will be in and out of the hospital on a regular basis before you know it."

Kaye marveled at how out of touch Rose was. It was her duty to educate her, right? "Rose, you're mistaken. Diabetes can be controlled quite successfully these days. Annie is a nurse, and she can fill you in. How can you not know that diabetes is very manageable?"

"Remember what I said, Kaye. You don't want to be a nurse or a purse. You'll see."

Kaye drove home muttering all the while about nosey, ignorant friends. Why did she let Rose get under her skin? Rose was a good person, but one with the major fault of needing to be right. Always. Why hadn't she just agreed with Rose's ridiculous assumption that Bob would need a caregiver soon?

Maybe she was worried that would be the case eventually. Did she want to nurse a man through a serious illness? She'd done that once with Stan and had been happy to do it. But it had been a serious strain. Sometimes Kaye still had nightmares about his cancer treatments and their effects. They'd had several good years together after that, though, until his fatal heart attack. It had all been worth it.

She resolved to give this dilemma to God, as she had so many others. God would guide her. She bent and turned to put her new nonstick cookie sheets in the narrow cupboard made for that purpose and was startled when her phone rang. She jumped to stand upright and rolled her ankle as she stood. Sweating with the sharp pain, she hobbled to the phone in the living room.

"Spam risk" was the reward for her effort. At least the cell phone carriers were getting better at identifying such nuisance calls. She sat down and propped her leg on the coffee table. Her ankle was already swollen. She remembered an elastic wrap in her bathroom closet and knew it would help, as would an ice pack. But she needed someone to get them for her.

Phone in hand, she called Bob. He arrived a few minutes later, clearly concerned. After helping her with the wrap and ice pack, he said, "This isn't good, Kaye."

"It's no big deal, Bob," Kaye said. "I'm just clumsy. Ice and pressure from the wrap are all I need. I'll be ready to bake with Katie in the morning."

Bob looked doubtful. "I don't agree. The swelling is pretty bad, and your ankle is starting to turn blue. Maybe we should go to the quick clinic for an X-ray."

"Absolutely not," Kaye retorted. "I'll be fine. Thanks for helping me with the wrap and ice. I've also got an old cane of Stan's in the hall closet from when he was sick." She shut her eyes and winced. "And maybe you could get me some pain reliever and a glass of water."

Bob complied with the cane and medication requests but still looked worried. "You shouldn't be alone, Kaye. What if you need to get up in the middle of the night? You can't walk without help."

Kaye made the effort to keep things light. "Bob, are you angling to stay the night? I'm not that kind of girl! As I said, I'll be fine. I've always had weak ankles. I rolled them almost daily when I was a kid." She was able to stand and hobbled to the television to retrieve the remote. "What's your viewing pleasure, Bob? We could watch the latest Netflix movie if you'd like."

"Sure, that's a good thought," Bob said. "Come sit next to me and we'll critique the latest in artistic filmmaking."

Kaye was suddenly very tired. She was also very grateful for Bob's presence. "Thanks, friend. You're the best."

Bob kissed her gently and nestled her head on his shoulder. "Just relax, Kaye. We'll get you taken care of tomorrow. But for now, let's enjoy the movie."

Five hours later, Kaye woke up with a start. "What's going on? Where am I? Why are you here, Bob?" She looked at her ankle, now propped up with a pillow and remembered. "I'm sorry, Bob. I've ruined your evening." She checked the time on her phone. "It's after midnight. You didn't have to stay with me." She made an attempt to stand and despite the cane, landed back on the sofa.

"I wanted to stay," Bob said. "It's time for you to take more pain relievers, and I'm guessing you could use some help getting to the bathroom. Let's get you freshened up and changed into a nightgown or whatever women your age sleep in. I plan to stay on the sofa until morning, just in case you need me."

Kaye was too tired to argue. Besides that, she knew Bob was right. She didn't want to be alone in the house. Her ankle was throbbing, she was parched, and she needed to use the bathroom. God was taking care of her while laughing at her plans for a quiet Sunday with her daughter, whose most pressing need was to learn to bake Christmas cookies.

Chapter Eleven

Katie surveyed her newly cleaned home. She'd taken care of Michelle's mess in the living room and her own in the disheveled kitchen. God had omitted the domestic gene when Katie had been born. She loved good food but couldn't prepare more than a helper-type dinner or a simple roasted chicken on her own. She was proud of her yard, though. Her dad had taught her how to mow and weed.

Kristen always insisted that cooking was like any other task requiring that directions be followed fairly closely. She also said that baking was more complex; with basic entree and side-dish recipes a person could take more risks. Baking though, was akin to a chemistry experiment, needing more precision and attention to detail.

Thankfully, her mother would be here soon. She'd help Katie figure out what to make as her entries for the cookie contest at GCC. No problem.

The doorbell rang and Katie answered. Kaye was leaning on a cane with Bob Benson propping her up on the other side.

"Mom! What's happened to you?" Katie was alarmed; her mother was never ill or injured. She'd been the rock when Dad was sick and later when he died. In a flash Katie realized how much her mother's strength mattered to her.

"I'm an awkward female," Kaye joked with a wince. "Bob has helped me since I hurt my ankle last evening. He wants me to get X-rayed, but I want to help you with your cookies."

"Bob's right, Mom," Katie said as she helped her mother to the recliner chair. "Your ankle is huge and very colorful." Looking at Bob, she continued. "Bob, thanks for taking care of my mom. You're a good man."

Bob looked visibly moved by Katie's comment, and she realized how nasty she'd been to him under her previous thin layer of cordiality. She was ashamed, fearful about her mother's injury, and determined to be a better person.

"Why don't we cancel our baking plans? There's a couple of weeks before the contest deadline. I can make do. Better yet, I can ask Kristen for help."

"No, I insist," Kaye announced. "I won't let my careless nature interfere with my life. Let's get going."

The next few hours resulted in the depletion of two bags of flour and almost as many bags of sugar. Pastry tips and bags were soiled, washed, and reused. Food coloring drips dotted Katie's quartz countertops. Each woman had flour in her hair and fingernails decked in festive Christmas colors.

Gingerbread humans were sloppily decorated, but delicious. Sugar cookie stars and bells were in the same condition, tasty but unattractive. Bob, being a good sport, had several cookies but quit after checking his blood sugar.

"Ladies, I think we should call it a day," he said. "It's past my lunchtime and cookies aren't on my meal plan. Kaye, you look tired and we're still going to get an X-ray, so we need to head out." He looked expectantly at Katie.

She picked up on Bob's signal. "Bob's right, Mom. You're tired and in pain. Don't think I haven't noticed the deep breathing you've been doing for the last half hour. Get to the clinic. It's an order from your youngest daughter!"

Kaye laughed. To Bob and Katie's surprise, she agreed. "I think you two are right. This ankle needs to be checked. I probably just need a brace for a few weeks, but it's best to be sure. Katie, you're making progress. The cookies are delicious!"

Katie hugged her mother. "Mom, only a mother could love these cookies. I'll freeze them and take them to an ugly Christmas sweater party. They'll fit right in." She looked at Bob. "Will you let me know what the doctor says? I don't trust Mom to give me the full scoop."

Bob agreed. Kaye scowled at him but accepted his help getting to the car. Katie kissed Kaye and said, "It's okay not to be tough all the time, Mom. Take help from those who love you."

As she waved Bob's car off, she realized Bob loved her mom. He wasn't the effusive type, but his worry lines each time Kaye moved said it all. He had it bad for her mother. Katie was suddenly aware she was fine with that. He was a better man than she'd realized. Again, God convicted her for her judgment.

Unable to focus on a book and bored with the

television offerings, she returned to the kitchen. Suddenly she remembered cornflake wreath cookies from her childhood. Mostly the memories involved green food coloring, but the cookies had been easy and delicious. Maybe she could make them on her own.

A quick internet search told her she'd have to hit the grocery again for mini marshmallows and some Red Hots candy. No problem. She needed groceries anyway.

Once at the no-frills store she loved and armed with her own grocery sacks, she forced herself to avoid the ready-made frozen food entrees and study the fresh meat and poultry counters. Surely she could bake chicken breasts, and with a simple steamed vegetable she'd have dinner ready. And Kristen was always making pasta with butter and parmesan cheese for Michelle. It sounded quite tasty to Katie. She'd always been leery of spicy food but buttery goodness was comforting to her.

So that made two dinners from scratch—baked chicken breasts with frozen broccoli and spaghetti with butter sauce. The rest of the week would be takeout or something from her frozen food stash in the garage freezer. She didn't want to go overboard with this cooking from scratch thing. Baby steps, she always said. Remembering why she originally made the trip, the cookie wreath ingredients were gathered and Katie made her way to the checkout line.

She heard her name and was shocked to see Louis. What was the gourmand doing at the bargain food store? She asked him that very question.

"Katie, Katie, Katie. You're such a snob without

knowing it. This place is full of treasures, all at good prices." Louis pointed to his cart, which revealed a whole salmon, multiple flavors of hummus, and whole grain, seeded bread. "I love this place. If I don't come weekly, I wonder what I've missed out on."

"I come often too," Katie replied. "But for the prices, not the exotic food."

Louis smiled that killer smile. Katie swooned a little, hoping he didn't notice. But his twinkling eyes revealed he did.

"Let's see what's in your cart," he teased. "Ah, marshmallows and cornflakes. Probably for wreath cookies, correct? They should fit well in the kid's category for the contest."

Katie fumed. *Of course* they would fit in the kid category. That had been her plan. But Louis' snooty condescension was too much. She knew she couldn't win a battle of cookie wits, so she didn't try. "Right, as always, Louis. That's my plan. Easy cookies that children can make memories with while they learn to navigate the kitchen."

"It's a good plan, Katie. Kids need to learn to cook and enjoy themselves while doing it. Today's children are so regimented with sports and music lessons that they miss out on the pleasures of nourishing themselves and those they love. What could be a better learning experience?"

"No argument here," Katie said. "I'd better let you get back to your shopping. I'm finished. Lots to do." She took a breath and decided to let Louis in on the day's events. "I'm also waiting on Bob Benson's call about my mother. She took a fall hurrying to answer the phone and is having her ankle X-rayed."

Louis' brows crunched. He looked truly sorry, which was a shock to Katie. "Katie, that's terrible. What can I do for your mom? Maybe cook her dinner and bring it to her place? I'd be glad to help."

Katie hugged Louis before she knew what she was doing. "That's lovely, but not necessary. Thanks for the thought."

"I'll call you tonight and check in," Louis said. "I want to know what's going on." After a beat, he added, "And what can I do for you? You look worried."

Well, you could come over and we could kiss on the wing chair without getting caught by my mom, Katie thought. *Then you could cook me a divine dinner and ply me with great wine. Who knows what else you could do?*

She shook away her fantasies and shrugged. "I'm good, Louis. But thanks again."

Bob helped Kaye as they entered her house. The cast reached to her right knee, completely encasing her lower leg and most of her foot. Only her hot pink toenails, courtesy of her recent pedicure, peaked out. She lowered herself into her favorite recliner and started to weep.

"Oh, honey, don't cry," Bob said, with a bit of fear in his voice. Evidently a broken ankle was less scary than a sixty-something woman crying softly in her living room. "The doc said you'd be fine in six or seven weeks. Until then, I'm your slave."

Kaye's tears increased. "Almost two months!" she wailed. "How will I function? These crutches are instruments of torture. My armpits are already sore. I'm going to need twenty-four-hour care."

She sniffed loudly. "And I can't afford that! All the commercials say Medicare won't pay for long-term care costs."

Bob looked at the woman he'd grown to love. Actually, he admitted to himself he'd cared for her even back when she'd rebuffed his stupid advances soon after Stan's death. He'd been an idiot—lonely and bereft himself, but still an idiot. It was time to set her straight.

"Look, lady, you have plenty of folks who will tend to you without having to enlist outside caregivers. I love you, your girls love you, and even Linda will help out." He arched his brows and added, "Linda will enjoy herself immensely as she watches you maneuver those crutches."

Kaye was forced to laugh. "You're right. Lots of people will help me." She looked down. "I may love you, too, Bob. I wasn't sure until now. You've been a good friend, which is all I've been telling myself. But it's more than that, isn't it?" She looked at him with a combination of wonder and horror.

Bob leaned over her chair and kissed her. Holding her hand, he replied, "Yes, we're more than friends. You look a little concerned, though. What's wrong with us being in love?"

Kaye tried to straighten herself in the chair. "We're too old for this stuff!" she said. "You heard that emergency doctor, who looks barely out of her teens, by the way. I've got old lady bones! You need someone younger than this old hen."

He started to laugh but stopped himself when he saw the real pain in Kaye's eyes. It was time for some tough love, maybe a little too soon after his declaration of romantic love, but Kaye was starting to get hysterical again. "Kaye Anderson, stop it. You've got bones that are a result of your age and genetic bad luck. The good thing is there's treatment for them. You'll be stronger than ever once the medicine works its magic."

Kaye finally released the slow smile that always unnerved him. "Okay, Bob Benson. I hear you. We need a plan, though. You can't just move in here."

"Why not?" he answered. "You've got an extra bedroom." He grinned. "Unless you want to share yours."

"Not going to happen," Kaye said. "I'm too old to be living in sin, especially in the hotbed of gossip Gordon Park has turned out to be. I guess you could stay some nights in the second bedroom until I'm able to take care of myself."

"I sure could," he said. "I was going to say you could give me more cooking lessons, but in all likelihood the meal train at church will kick in and we'll each gain ten pounds before your cast is off."

"And then I'll need physical therapy!" Kaye shouted. "I won't be able to drive myself to those appointments either, since it's my right ankle that's broken." Kaye stopped herself and added, "However, one of my friends in Phoenix managed to use her left foot on both the gas pedal and brake with her right leg over the console. Do you think I could manage that?"

Horrified at the thought of Kaye driving in such a dangerous manner, Bob cringed. "If you don't settle down, I'm going to have to use your full name again," he said. "Cut it out, Kaye. You'll have plenty of drivers to PT. But first, we have to talk about this 'living in sin' you're so worried about."

Kaye studied him. "It will be okay for you to be in the guest room," she said quietly. "But not for long.

Living together works for some, but not for me. I've always been a woman who needed a firm pledge from a man."

"Doesn't saying we love each other count?" Bob asked. "One of my mall-walking buddies had a commitment ceremony with his fiancée and they exchanged rings to mark the occasion. It was just like a wedding, but kept their assets separate for their grown kids. Makes sense to me."

"A commitment ceremony? Who conducted it? Your friend's beer buddy who got ordained a few minutes before on the internet? Sorry, but that's a 'no' from me."

Kaye was getting worked up again. "What kind of commitment does a couple have that prohibits marriage? Don't they have prenups, or trusts, or whatever to protect assets?" She shrugged and grimaced at the pain in her leg. "What are we even talking about, anyway? I need a nap. You need to go. I'll call Katie to bring me some supper and she can help me at bedtime. Thanks for everything, Bob."

Bob knew when his beloved was at the end of her rope. Reasoning with her would be futile. He'd call Katie and fill her in. If she had to let him in after Kaye fell asleep, she would. He didn't want Kaye to be alone. Hopefully, Katie would understand.

Louis pulled up to Katie's house. He ambled up the sidewalk, noting her neatly trimmed bushes and flowering plants. The woman couldn't function in the kitchen, but her yard looked nice. Before he could ring the bell, she opened the door.

Motioning for him to be quiet, she pointed to the

phone in her hand and spoke with a harried tone. "I know, Mom, it's very upsetting," she said. "You'll heal, despite your 'old lady bones'. Bob said he loved you? Wow, that's news. And you said it back? Who said you have to live in sin? I'm confused."

Louis watched as Katie listened to her mother's disjointed conversation. Poor Katie. She had enough to deal with at work (which was partially his fault, he admitted to himself), and with Kristen's step-kid. Now her mother was injured and from the sound of things, not dealing with it well.

"Sure, I'll bring you supper and help you get ready for bed. I'll see you in half an hour." Katie ended the call and shot a glance at Louis.

"What brings you by, Louis? I thought you'd call to check on Mom's status."

"I was about to lie and say I was in the neighborhood," he said. "But I wanted to see you. I'm glad I stopped by. I take it Kaye's not in the best shape?"

"No, she has a broken ankle, a cast, and crutches that she can't handle. She and Bob are professing their love, but he only wants to move in, not marry her." Motioning for Louis to sit, Katie continued. "There's obviously more going on than what I just told you, but that's my mother. When she's stressed, everything crumbles apart in her mind. Kaye Anderson is the master of the worst-case scenario."

Louis ached for Katie. He moved next to her in the wing chair, surprised that she seemed to welcome him in. There was more going on with Katie then he'd thought. After a long kiss, he said, "Let me whip up some supper from the groceries I spotted in your cart earlier and we'll both go to see your mom."

While he cooked, Katie filled him in on the phone call she'd received from Bob, just before Kaye had called. Bob's plan to stay in the house with Kaye overnight had merit. Louis said as much.

"I agree," Katie said. "I just don't feel right deceiving Mom and sneaking Bob in after she's in bed. What if she thinks he's a prowler? I've got to be honest with her."

"You're right on both counts. Your mother shouldn't be alone, and she should know about Bob's presence. We'll convince her, you'll see."

After cooking for barely twenty minutes, Louis drove Katie to her mother's. Kaye and Bob were delighted with the lemon chicken breasts and the sides Louis had gleaned from Katie's meager pantry. He hated using the instant mashed potatoes but fancied them up with sour cream and cheddar cheese.

Sensing her mother was in a better mood, Katie made her pitch for Bob to stay the night. "Mom, you look tons better than when we arrived. How are you feeling?"

"I'm better, as you say," Kaye replied. "The pain meds are kicking in. I'll be fine tonight. Bob can come by in the morning."

Louis looked at Katie. Her face transformed into that thunderous look he knew so well.

"No, Mom, Bob isn't going to leave. I talked to Kristen and we're going to alternate nights with you. Counting Bob, that's every third night that we'll be with you. Kristen can manage with Michelle here; that kid sleeps anywhere. Your guest room and the den with the sofa bed are going to get a workout, which is why you bought this particular house plan."

Kaye looked alternately rebellious, furious, and resigned. Louis was glad to see resignation take hold. "Fine, I'll allow it. Bob has been telling me it's okay to ask for help. I do need it right now. But we'll take it week by week, agreed? Surely I won't need babysitting for six weeks."

"Probably not, but we'll take it a bit at a time," Katie said. She looked at Louis for confirmation.

Pleased that she seemed to be asking for his input, he said, "Kaye, you're a gutsy woman. But what strikes me as more impressive is how much your family and Bob care for you. Six weeks will fly by, and you'll be back walking with your friends each morning."

Louis drove Katie home and made a quick exit. But not before he planted quick kisses on her lips and neck as they lingered on her tiny porch. He was hesitant about her offer to come in, and finally said, "I'd better not, Katie. You're much too tempting tonight, full of emotion and concern for your mom. My instinct is to soothe you in any way I can, which would start by cozying up on that wing chair. Probably not a good idea."

Katie agreed, a little. She wanted Louis to come in but knew he was right. She was a jumble of feelings. Worried about her mother, somewhat skeptical of Bob's seeming devotion, and longing for Louis in a way she hadn't felt in quite a while. Even Dan hadn't caused this much longing. They'd been almost engaged, but never passionate or full of lust. And her feelings for Glenn had been almost maternal as he dealt with his divorce. There was nothing maternal about what she felt for Louis! She'd have to be careful.

Too wired to read or sleep, she decided to try the cornflake cookie wreath recipe. After microwaving the cornflakes and marshmallows, she added the green food coloring and vanilla and stirred with all her might. Too much might, as it happened. She ended up with a shredded mess.

Lesson learned. She used a gentler approach with the second batch and dropped the cookie lumps onto wax paper. By the time she tried to separate the lumps into wreath shapes, they'd hardened into little cookie balls. At this rate, she'd need more cornflakes and marshmallows soon.

Hating to waste good ingredients, she thought about ways to salvage the gooey green shapes. Remembering the tube of sugar cookie dough in the refrigerator, she let it soften to room temperature for ten minutes. Louis had told her once, in his superior way, that cold dough was good for cutting cookies into shapes, but room temperature was better for rolling into one big mass.

Katie rolled the dough into a circle (or a shape resembling one) and put the cornflake clumps around the edge of the circle. Using premade frosting, she "glued" the cornflake chunks to the circle. She added RedHots to simulate holly berries and pleased with the effect, baked it all according to the cookie wrapper directions.

This experiment was also a disaster. The dough baked up perfectly, but the cornflake wreaths were burned to an appetite-killing shade of brown. Now she needed to buy more premade cookie dough, frosting, cornflakes, and marshmallows. The GCC cookie contest was becoming expensive but she was determined to prevail. Tomorrow. For now, Katie was beyond fatigued and ready for bed.

Sunday dawned bright and clear. After checking in with her mother and confirming Kaye's positive report with Bob's input, Katie was determined to perfect her entries for the cookie competition. A quick trip to the store, two hours of cooking, and a successful test of buckeye candy did the trick.

So what if buckeyes were technically candies and not cookies? Her dad had been born in Ohio and they were a tribute to him. Not to mention that the buckeyes required little mixing, no baking, and zero frosting. Melting chocolate for the outer layer was a snap with the microwave. She was careful about that, because numerous recipes cautioned to watch the chocolate closely lest it separate from overheating. The buckeyes would be the perfect entry for the easy recipe category. The huge cornflake wreaths (now baked properly), one made with a circle of sugar cookie dough and one with chocolate chip, would surely place in the kid's category.

Katie compiled a plate of sweets for her mother. Bob shouldn't eat many of them, but she wanted to thank him for staying with her mother last night. On her way to Kaye's, she stopped at a minimart and purchased a gift card for Bob to use the next time he shopped for groceries. He was certainly a surprise.

Far removed from the man who had jumped to ask Kaye out when she was a new widow, he seemed to be a person of humility and substance. Maybe his own brush with diabetes had changed him. Or maybe he had been grieving when he asked Kaye for a date. Katie had a flash of them kissing, quickly shaking the image out of her thoughts. Some things were better left out of the imagination!

She pulled up to Kaye's house when her phone rang. Sitting in the car, she answered, "Good morning, Louis. What's going on?"

"That's my question for you," he said. "How was your mom's night? How are you? Did you get any sleep?"

"We're both doing fine," Katie answered with a smile. "Thanks again for all your help yesterday. You'll be proud to know I've been cooking all morning. I've perfected my two entries for the contest."

"Two entries? I thought the cornflake cookies were it."

"A secret twist on cornflake cookies is one entry. And buckeyes are the second! They're really yummy. Chocolate and peanut butter are the perfect ingredient combo, Louis."

Her proud announcement was greeted with a long silence. Finally, Louis said, "Katie, you're a sweetheart, but you know buckeyes are a candy, right? I'm not sure the judges will accept them."

"Yes, I know they're candies," Katie said. Well, she'd known for about a half hour, when she'd looked at the title of the recipe more closely. "But everyone I know has them on their cookie trays at the holidays. The judges will understand."

"You're something, Katie. You're probably right.

Congrats on finishing your entries. I'm still working on mine."

"Need any help?" Katie asked, dissolving into a long chuckle.

Louis chuckled back. "I might," he answered. "It would be fun to have you over while the cookies bake. We could fill the time with no problem, I'm sure."

They joined in a chorus of laughter, Katie wondering and hoping Louis' idea of filling time matched hers.

"But on to other things. I made another meal for your mom, Katie. I hope she likes beef stew. When would be a good time for me to drop the food off?"

"I'm in front of her house as we speak," Katie said. "Mom loves beef stew. Unless you're talking about the kind in a can. I'm puzzled at how you found the time to make it."

Appalled, Louis almost shouted into the phone. "A can! Woman, you can't be serious! My beef stew is entirely homemade. It's also very efficient because I used the slow cooker all night to tenderize the beef."

"My apologies," Katie said, with minimal repentance in her voice. "So, are you coming over now?"

"I'll be right there. After we visit with your mom, we'll have a chat on our own." He paused and added, "A can!"

"There won't be any private chats for us tonight. It's my turn to stay with mom, remember? I'm here until tomorrow morning."

"You're a good daughter," Louis said with a groan. "But you have to work on your girlfriend role. It needs some help."

"I'm your girlfriend? I'll have to think about that."

After a few seconds, she said, "I've thought about it. I like it a lot, *boyfriend.* See you soon."

Louis' response was a simple, "Yes, I'm your boyfriend, but only because there's no better term. We aren't lovers, and partner sounds too business-like. I'll work on it."

Arriving in under ten minutes, Louis walked Katie to her mother's front door. The scene greeting them was interesting. Kaye looked fresh, with her leg propped up on a pillow on the coffee table. Bob looked like a truck had hit him.

"How lovely to see you two," Kaye said. "And Louis, what's the divine smell coming from that bowl?"

"Beef stew, with some additions of my own. Wine, pearl onions, button mushrooms, thyme, that sort of thing."

Katie snorted. "Even I know that's not beef stew, Louis. It's beef bourguignon, isn't it? Why not just be honest? You're showing off!"

Everyone laughed, and Louis admitted his deception. "I've also brought some homemade egg noodles to serve with the casserole," he said. "You and Bob should be able to eat on this for a few meals."

Kaye expressed her gratitude. Bob looked almost weak in relief. "Thanks, Louis. I was a little frantic trying to plan the next few suppers."

"Mom, how are you feeling?" Katie asked.

"I'm fine, really. My leg is sore, but manageable with the over-the-counter meds." Kaye looked at Bob, adding, "He, on the other hand, looks terrible. I doubt he slept all night."

"Bob, thanks for taking such good care of Mom," Katie said. "Why don't we all have some of Louis' 'stew' and you can hit the road for your place. I'm here for the rest of the night, and I don't have to be at work tomorrow until after ten."

Katie smiled at Bob's obvious sigh of happiness. "And Kristen is on for overnight duty tomorrow tonight. Therefore, Mom won't need you until Tuesday evening."

Bob grimaced. "I will definitely be here tomorrow at ten," he said. "Your mother is a strong woman, but I want to be sure she's not overdoing it."

Katie waited for Kaye's explosion, but it didn't come. Instead, her mother was looking at Bob with tears in her eyes while Bob held her hands in his. Good grief. Those two were crushing like seventh graders. Wait until Kristen got wind of this!

Chapter Twelve

Louis practiced his stained-glass cookies in the food lab after classes on Monday. The basic recipe was almost insulting in its simplicity. Roll out the sugar cookie dough (his was homemade, naturally), cut out the basic shape, and then cut out the smaller echo shape to fill in later with crushed hard candies. He wanted to fancy the cookies up by using petit four frosting on the outside shape, to add flavor and increase the difficulty. He was the director of the culinary arts program, after all.

Director or not, figuring out how to add the frosting was no easy task. If he added it first, then baked in the hard candy, it burned. When he frosted the completed cookies, the icing didn't cooperate, instead running all over the candy centers on most of the cookies. After a few hours of experimenting, he thickened the frosting with just enough royal icing to make it workable. The cookies were pieces of art. Grabbing his phone, he called Katie.

"Hullo?" she answered, deep in the fog of sleep. "Louis, what's going on? It's after one in the morning."

"It is? I'm sorry. I've been working on my stained-glass cookies and didn't realize. They finally turned out the way I wanted." Louis envisioned Katie in bed, all messy and rumpled, half asleep. He liked the mental picture. It would be better if he were with her, of course. He'd have her awake in no time.

"Good for you," Katie said. "Anything else?"

"No, that's it. I wanted to tell you first thing. Sleep tight, girlfriend."

Katie laughed and disconnected. He wondered if she'd remember the call. Despite waking her, he was glad he'd talked to her. He couldn't get enough of her lately.

After classes on Tuesday, Louis continued to experiment with the stained-glass cookies. He fashioned some of the sturdier cookies into ornaments by poking a hole in the top prior to baking, thinking he'd complete his entry with a small Christmas tree decorated with his baked confections. He'd brought a miniature artificial tree from home and set to work. Italian wedding cakes were nestled into the branches, along with dark, peppermint, and white chocolate bark. A gingerbread family, linking hands with red ribbon, decorated the front. The little tree looked somewhat Charlie Brownish, but he liked the effect.

"Oooh, that's pretty," Katie said from behind his shoulder. "I'm jealous I didn't think to decorate a tree as part of my entry." She circled the tree. "You know, my buckeyes would look good in between the branches too. Kind of like nuts for the squirrels. Would you like me to donate some to your cause?"

After giving her a quick kiss, he said, "Only if

you let me credit you in my display. That's nice of you, Katie."

"As your official girlfriend, of course I'm nice to you," Katie said, batting her lashes. "And my boyfriend has been very nice to me and my family. That so-called 'beef stew' was over-the-top, you know. Bob looked like he might ask you to marry him, but he's already asked Mom."

"What?! Did Kaye accept his proposal?"

"They're still haggling. Bob's proposal was more of a 'let's live together after a commitment ceremony' type of thing. Mom's very traditional, so it didn't fly. Kristen and I are taking bets on who wins."

Katie stared at the tree and continued. "You know, I was on board with Mom and Bob being a couple when I saw how much he cared for her. Even before her fall, when Mom was giving Bob cooking tips, he was obviously in love with her. And Mom resisted Rose Dolce's interference about Bob from the first, so she must have felt something for him. Kristen, however, the daughter who has professed her forgiveness for Bob *way* before I did, has reservations. Weird, huh?"

Louis took Katie's hand. "Love is hard to figure out sometimes, both for ourselves and others. Maybe Kristen's trouble with Sophie and her distance from Mike are adding to the mix. Knowing you as I do, I sense a plan in the works. What's your next move?"

"My plan is to keep my nose out of this." Noting Louis' arched brows, she added, "Hard to believe, I know. But right now, I want to focus on my own love life."

Louis walked to the classroom door and locked it. "Excellent plan, Katie. Let's focus."

Several minutes later, with Katie in the rumpled, messy state he decided he enjoyed immensely, they left the food lab.

"What are you up to now, Katie? Want to grab a bite?"

"Sure," she answered. "I don't know if baking counts as cooking, but after this contest I'm done in the kitchen for a while. Restaurant food is sounding better and better."

"Well, it doesn't hold a candle to what I can make for you, but I agree. I'm ready for someone else to cook for a while." Louis directed Katie to his car. "How about that little diner? Would that work for you?"

"Ah, the scene of our fight," Katie said with a grin. "Was it our first or one of many? I can't remember."

"One of many, I think. I'm glad we're past that phase."

"Me, too." Katie smiled and squeezed his thigh. "This is much better."

Kaye studied Bob as he slept in the recliner. Kristen was due in an hour. Bob would have to go home, finally. His steady concern was endearing, but a bit stifling. She knew she was being hypocritical, though. If he'd been in a cast, she'd be acting the same way.

What was it about Bob that caused her to resist his kindness, his love? Was it Bob himself or another factor? Suddenly, she thought of a conversation she'd had with a cousin many years ago. They'd been discussing their aging parents and their worries about them taking care of themselves. Kaye remembered saying, "It's like my mom and dad together equal one well-functioning person. They can't do it alone anymore."

That was it. The notion that she and Bob might only amount to one fully autonomous person terrified her. Her gut told her the idea had some truth; she'd been Bob's caregiver when his diabetes had been out of control and now, he was her rock while she needed crutches. Was this the beginning of the end? Would she be in a nursing facility before she knew it? Her eyes burned.

Bob stirred, awakened by Kaye's quiet sobs. "Honey, what's wrong?" he asked, rubbing the sleep out of his eyes. "Are you in pain? Is your leg swollen?"

"I'm fine," Kaye said, standing over him. She turned away, trying to undo the damage to her face the tears had caused. But this was Bob. She had no reason to hide her feelings. She turned to him and said, "Okay, I'm not fine. I love you, but I hate the reality that I depend on you. That you depend on me." She choked back a wail. "We're old, Bob! What's going to become of us?"

Bob smiled that soothing smile she'd come to rely on. Funny, she relied on his emotional stability as much as on his help with the crutches. She realized she'd depended on Stan for much the same thing— the centering and the calming influence during those times when she melted down.

"What's going to become of us is that we'll have a fine time together as your ankle heals and as I deal with whatever else God throws at me." He studied her stricken face. "Yes, we're getting old, Kaye. It's hard to deny. You're at the end of your sixties and I'm into my seventies. But look at all the fun we've had despite our age. We laugh, we bicker, and we even cook together. I enjoy your kids and grand-kids, though you've yet to meet mine. They've been nagging me to bring you by. We'll fix that when you can take a long car ride to Evansville. And to top all that, soon we'll enjoy the added benefits of being a married couple. Right?" He leered at Kaye and she was forced to laugh.

"I thought you wanted to commit, not marry," Kaye said with an edge to her tone. "You said we needed to protect our assets for our kids."

"I did say that," Bob admitted. "But upon reflection, I don't want Rose Dolce to give you a hard time about being a scarlet woman." Bob kissed her and managed to maneuver her onto his lap. "Wow, this cast is heavy, Kaye. But I like having you here. It's where you need to be. Where I need you to be."

"You do? You need to be with me when I'm crying and spiraling out of control with my doomsday thoughts?" She shifted in the chair to take the weight of her cast off Bob's lap. "It's okay to take what you just said back, you know."

"I'm not taking anything back. My wife used to say I ignored her feelings when they struck too close to home. I'm determined to do better by you. Of course, you'll have to do some things differently, too."

"What? What do I need to change?"

"My dear, you need to work on trusting yourself. You're a kind, responsible, loving woman. People like Rose will always be free with their advice, but your heart is a good guidepost. Follow it."

Kaye nestled in. Bob held her close and they sealed their new engagement with a long kiss, enjoying all the feelings involved with trust and risk. Kaye thought there was no better place to be. Stan had been her first love, her sweetheart from high school. Bob was different, but still a true love.

As they enjoyed exploring their feelings for each other, Kaye's doorbell rang, and Kristen let herself in. Stuck in Bob's lap by the weight of her cast and his firm grip on her, she smiled at her daughter.

Kristen was not smiling. "What's this, Mom? I thought Bob was at his place. It's my night to stay, correct?"

"Bob's been kind enough to stay with me today," Kaye said. "I really appreciate his company. And I'm looking forward to your company tonight and in the morning."

"Let me help you out of this chair," Kristen grumbled. "You look very uncomfortable. Bob, thanks for your attention to Mom. But I'm sure you've got things to do." Kristen looked pointedly at the door.

Bob got the hint, not that it was much of a hint. It was more like a directive. He managed a quick kiss on Kaye's cheek before Kristen edged her off the recliner. He was halfway to the foyer when Kaye spoke.

"Kristen, you're being rude. Bob has been my salvation through all this. And as he's my fiancé, you need to treat him with respect."

"Your WHAT?" Kristen bellowed. "Mom, have you lost your mind? What about how he treated you and me just a few years ago? How can you trust this guy?"

"As I recall, you recently gave me a lecture on forgiveness. I've forgiven Bob, and I thought you had as well. What's changed?"

"I've forgiven him as a colleague and acquaintance, and maybe as your commitment partner, but not as your husband-to-be. We'll have to discuss this tonight, Mom. We need a long talk."

"No, Kristen, we don't need to talk alone tonight. We can talk now, and you can voice your concerns to both Bob and me." "I will speak to you alone or with my sister present," Kristen said. "Otherwise, I'm leaving."

Kaye stood silent, with a white-knuckle grasp on her crutches. Kristen turned on her heel, picked up her overnight tote, and left. Minutes later, Kaye heard the squeal of her tires as she drove off.

"I'm sorry, Kaye," Bob said. "I'll leave and you can call her on her cell phone. She can turn around and come right back here."

"Absolutely not," Kaye said. "I love my daughter, but she's not going to dictate my life choices. Aren't you the person who just said I needed to trust myself when others offered unsolicited advice?"

"I am," Bob said. "But who's going to stay with you tonight?"

"Why you are, of course," Kaye said. "Get back in that recliner and let's continue where we left off."

The week at GCC culminated with the staff/faculty meeting on Friday at five, scheduled as always the week before final exams. It was devoid of the typical business and scholarly committee reports, solely an excuse for a party during which the Christmas cookies were judged.

Katie was dressed in her best ugly Christmas sweater, taking lots of ribbing from her colleagues.

Kristen noticed the attention directed at Katie but smiled. Katie thought her sister looked tense. No wonder, given the thrashing she'd given her mother and Bob a few days ago. Louis, oblivious to Christmas fashion and not caring what Katie wore, told her she looked wonderful.

After a wordy rehash of the contest rules, the chairperson of the cookie contest announced the winners to general applause. Everyone was anxious to get to the real purpose of the meeting—taking one of each entered cookie home to their families and friends. Louis was delighted to win first prize for his stained-glass ornament cookies in the gourmet category. He'd been sure to explain the difficult process for frosting them. He was shocked to earn second place in the kid-friendly category (which he hadn't even entered) for his decorated Christmas tree. He looked at Katie and mouthed "What did you do?"

Katie grinned, basking in her first-place prize in the kid-friendly category. Those darned cornflake wreaths had paid off. She'd spent almost the equivalent of a week's grocery budget getting them right, but it was worth it. And who cared that the buckeyes weren't technically cookies? Evidently no one, since they earned third place in the easy category. After a tough first semester, she finally felt that she belonged at GCC. She was no longer Kristen's little sister, or Louis' nemesis/girlfriend, but a professional and a coworker in her own right. Marveling at how much this contest meant to her, she found Louis chatting with the faculty from the psychology department.

Kristen saw Katie and pulled her away. "How's Mom doing?" she asked. "I've called her, and she gives me terse answers. Is she really okay?"

Katie studied her normally composed sister. "She's not lying, Sis. Her leg is healing well. She's able to do more now that she knows how to deal with the crutches." Katie studied Kristen and took a leap. "Bob is helping her a lot. He's good for her. It's not only the caregiving, Kristen, it's his love. He calms her down and gives her hope. That's what we all want, right?"

"Right," Kristen said, as tears filled her eyes. "I agree, despite what you may think. Mike gave me an earful about my attitude toward Bob. Then I gave him an earful about his spoiled daughter."

Katie's eyes bugged out. "I'm sorry things are still rough," she said. "What can I do? Would it help if the girls stayed with me this weekend? Maybe you and Mike could work things out."

Kristen laughed, and her tension faded. "No, it's fine. We've worked things out, all right. After the biggest fight of our marriage, I agreed that I've been a baby about Mom remarrying and Mike agreed that Sophie needs some serious boundaries. And as I always tell my Counseling 101 students, boundaries eventually help all the parties involved. Sophie is actually relieved that her dad is standing up to her."

Katie hugged her sister, knowing the full story was much more complicated than Kristen was admitting. That was okay. Kristen seemed to be in a better place. "I'm so happy to hear this," Katie said. "Now you have to talk to Mom and Bob. To use your parlance, you have to admit that Mom has a right to set boundaries, too."

"You're right," Kristen said as she put on her coat. "You might want to consider a second master's in counseling. Have a great weekend, Katie."

Louis strolled over and watched Kristen leave. "Everything okay with your sister?" he asked. "And with your Mom?"

"Things are just dandy," she said. "Congrats on your awards, Louis. You did yourself proud."

"As did you," Louis said, squeezing her hand. "I'll admit, I never thought you'd place in any of the categories."

Feeling slightly injured, Katie let it go. "But I did, didn't I? I gave this silly contest my all. And do you know why?"

Louis looked puzzled. "Because you love competition? Because you love desserts? And Christmas? And me?"

Katie gasped. Did she love Louis? She loved calling him her boyfriend. She loved his kindness toward her mother. She loved his concern about Kristen. She loved his sexy manner, his temperamental chef's attitude, and his ability to render her senseless when he kissed her. Did that mean she loved *him*?

"I just might love you," she answered slowly. "It's a little scary, though. You're a world-famous chef, with a romantic history light years ahead of mine. I may be in over my head."

"This is no place to discuss matters of the heart," Louis mumbled. "Let's get out of here. We're headed to my place, in my car. I'll drop you off later to get yours."

Once at Louis' home, they settled on floor pillows beside the fire he'd started. "Katie Anderson, I love you. I'm annoyed you don't know that, but it's my fault. To be honest, I've been determined not to be a phony when it comes to love, and I've not been open about my feelings for you. My time in England taught me lots about relationships, none of it good.

He paused and sipped his wine, edging closer to Katie. "In fact, relationships in the set I ran with were based almost on a currency model. 'What can this man or woman do for my image and career? If we attend this party, will our pictures make it to the pages of *Tattler*?' With you, I can be myself."

Katie rolled her eyes. "Yes, I agree. You're always yourself. You lecture me, you educate me about your notion of a quality internship, you scorn my Christmas cookies, all that."

Louis laughed. "Very true. I'm sorry if I've hurt you. But you've educated me, too. I'd best sum it up as a refresher course on Godly Midwestern values and all they encompass. My parents have been worried about me for years, and I think that values thing has been their biggest concern. They thought I was losing my sense of what was truly important in life." He kissed Katie, long and hard. "You are what's most important to me, Katie. My time in Europe seems like a bad dream compared to what we have together."

Katie took the initiative this time, cupping Louis' face in her hands. "You're a fine man, Louis. A little too handsome for your own good, smart as they come, and sweet at your core. You scare me to death." Her slow, lingering kiss belied his hard passion from a few moments before. "Let's take things slow, since we're both new at this approach to love."

"What new approach? If you love someone, that's it, right?"

"In the past, I've loved in a safe way, first with a man who was considered a good match for me. After that, I guess I loved a guy who needed me to hold his hand while he desired someone else. This time, I love you for you, with my fragile heart on the line if our relationship fails. As I said, it's scary."

"I'm determined not to frighten you, Katie. On the contrary. Let's just enjoy the fire. This relationship isn't going to fail."

Later, Katie drove home after Louis left her next to her car in the GCC lot. Yes, she loved him. *He loved her,* she thought. She'd have to trust him on that, which was her biggest challenge.

Her cell phone rang as she pulled into her driveway. "Louis, did you butt dial me?" she teased.

"No, I wanted to know if you made it home," he answered. "I'm suddenly very protective of you. You've got me all tangled up, Katie."

She smiled to herself. He did love her. *Thank you, Lord.*

Chapter Thirteen

Kaye continued to recover. Christmas was approaching fast. Her usual holiday style (to go over-the-top with everything from food to gifts) wasn't possible this year. Instead of time spent shopping and cooking, she was being ferried by Bob to physical therapy appointments with the goal of walking without a limp when her hated cast finally came off. She was also enjoying visits from her friends. Today Rose was coming over. Kaye sent Bob home. There was no need for him to endure whatever Rose had to say.

Her doorbell rang right on time. Rose was never late. Kaye was determined to be nice but in control. "Hi, Rose. It's sweet of you to come and visit me. I'm sure you're busy with Christmas being so close." "I felt it was my duty," Rose said, as she put a baked spaghetti casserole in Kaye's refrigerator. She settled into the chair by the fireplace.

Bob had insisted on starting a fire, saying it would lend a warm ambiance to the time Rose spent visiting. Kaye wasn't convinced.

"Duty? Whatever do you mean, Rose?"

"You've been my friend for longer than I can remember, Kaye. And you need a true friend at this time in your life. I'm worried you're about to make a huge mistake."

Kaye bristled. "Mistake? Again, what do you mean, Rose?"

"You know what I mean. Bob Benson has practically moved in. I hope to high heaven he's not convinced you to make a long-term commitment. There's nothing but pain in that scenario."

Wondering what Rose had heard, Kaye shifted in her seat. Stupid fire. Bob's goal for a sweet visit with the fire gently crackling in the background was a dismal failure.

"I'm not sure my relationship with Bob is any of your affair, Rose. We are friends, very good friends. And my girls like him, which is all that matters to me in terms of seeking others' approval."

"Affair. Good choice of words, Kaye. You're cohabitating with a man who's not your husband, or even your fiancé. What would Stan think?"

Kaye was furious. It was hard to stay in control when she wanted to strangle Rose Dolce.

"I'm at a loss for words, Rose. I thought you were my friend. Perhaps you should leave before we say things we'll regret." Kaye stood, held her crutches firmly, and waved to the front door. "You can let yourself out."

Rose's surprise at being challenged worked itself throughout her body. Shock lined her face, her shoulders shook, and she stumbled as she rose from her seat. After gathering herself, she sat back down and said, "Kaye, Kaye, my friend! There's no need for us to argue. I'm just trying to do what's best for you."

"Or best for you," Kaye said quietly as she returned to her chair. "What's best for you, Rose, seems to be to interfere with your friends' lives instead of asking them how they're doing, how they're handling frightening changes in their health." Kaye blew out a frustrated sigh. "And despite your purported concern for me and my family, I've yet to hear any expression of love for me. All I get from you is condemnation."

To Kaye's surprise, tears flowed down Rose's cheeks. After swiping them away, Rose got up and hugged Kaye, a massive effort since Kaye was seated and weighed down by her cast.

"Annie was right," Rose said. "She warned me, over and over, to be your friend, not your judge. I'm just worried, Kaye. Can you trust Bob?"

Kaye squinted at Rose. "Obviously, I do trust him. He's been my *best friend* since I broke my ankle." Kaye's meaning was not lost on Rose.

"Yes, I've been a bad friend. You've been on my mind constantly, but that's not helpful to you, is it? In my defense, Annie and Ben have been having a tough time trying to have a child. She's been referred to some sort of fertility guru in Indianapolis." Rose retrieved a tissue from her purse and cleaned up her face. "I guess since I can't control what they're going through, I thought I could help you make a good decision about Bob."

"You mean since you can't control what Annie's going through, you'd try to control me."

"I didn't mean it that way," Rose said softly. "But yes, that's what it amounts to. I'm sorry."

"Please tell Annie and Ben they're in my prayers,"

Kaye said. "Do you have any other questions?"

Rose's abject glance pleaded for forgiveness. "I shouldn't but I can't help myself. Are you and Bob engaged?"

"Yes, we are," Kaye said. "I'm not sure if that makes you feel better or worse about things, but I don't care."

Visibly fighting her need to comment, Rose said, "I'm happy if you are, Kaye. I mean that. And your girls accept him, which is all that matters." Rose looked at the fire for a few minutes. "Can we start over?"

Hating that she and her friend were at odds, Kaye nodded.

"So, how are you doing? Are you in pain? What can I do to help?"

"I'm doing well, Rose. My cast will be off soon, and physical therapy will help before and after the transition to a cane. Bob and I plan to go to Evansville to meet his kids after the first of the year." Noting Rose's questioning look, she added, "No, we haven't set a date yet. Probably early spring."

Almost back to her overbearing self, Rose asked, "Any jewelry I should see?"

"Not yet," Kaye answered. Enough was enough. Time to end this trying visit. "I'm getting tired, Rose. I'm overdue for a nap. Thanks so much for coming by. And thanks for the casserole. Bob and I will enjoy it this evening." Kaye knew she was poking the bear. Rose deserved it.

Rose left after a lingering hug. Despite Kaye's exhaustion, she grabbed her phone and called Linda. Rose's insight into the details of her relationship with Bob had to have come from Kaye's neighbor.

Time for another confrontation. Two in one day was more than Kaye could imagine. But she was angry.

"Hi, Kaye," Linda answered. "How are things?"

"I need you to come over. Now," Kaye said.

"I'll be right there. I'm so glad you called. I hope you're okay."

Kaye hung up.

Linda let herself in in response to Kaye's invitation. "Kaye, what's wrong? Did you fall?"

Kaye simply pointed to the chair recently vacated by Rose. "We need to talk."

Linda sat down, the lines in her forehead creasing deeply.

"Rose just left, as I'm sure you know," Kaye said. "She was full of concern for me. My worry is that her concern was fueled by your input."

"My input? What do you mean?"

"Rose knew all about Bob's visits. You're my neighbor. I thought we were friends, but my sense is you've been more of a spy than a friend lately."

"No, that's all wrong!" Linda protested. "I'm not spying. I can't help but notice Bob's car in your drive all the time. Neighbors look out for each other."

"Yes, they do. But they don't report to other people about what they see if nothing is amiss. Bob is helping me through a tough time. Anything beyond that is my business. I'm sure you can agree with that."

"Of course!" Linda regrouped and decided to go for more. "Are you two getting closer? Any future plans I should know about?"

"Nope, nothing you need to know," Kaye said. Pointing to the door, she added, "Thanks for stopping by and letting me clear this up, Linda. I'll call when I want to talk. No need to call me."

Linda left and Kaye was alone. She was proud of standing up to two busybodies in one morning. Because she'd always liked pretty rings, and because she was still enough of a traditionalist to want a sparkler on her finger, Rose's question about jewelry nagged at her. But Bob was a good man and that was all that mattered. She composed a group text to Bob, Kristen, Mike, Katie, and Louis:

I have a mountain of baked spaghetti casserole in the fridge. Let's have a family get-together (bring the kids) this evening. Short notice, but you won't have to cook!

The text responses started to flow in, all accepting her invitation for the impromptu dinner. Kaye sat at the kitchen table and threw together a spinach salad from produce she had on hand. She thawed and buttered a baguette for garlic bread. Proud again, she had to credit her physical therapist. She'd made the sides for dinner! Once the horrendous cast was off, she'd be functional again. *Thanks be to God.*

The dinner was a huge success. Kaye's family members were relaxed, and Kristen almost catered to Bob in an effort to make peace. Since Sophie was at a sleepover and Michelle was with the sitter, Kristen asked him about dealing with a preteen daughter.

"I'm far past that stage of parenting," he admitted. "But I do recall that the calmer I stayed, the better the outcome. I also did a lot of praying with my wife when our daughters were at that age."

"I didn't realize you were religious," Kristen said. "That helps me. I hate to admit it, but my concern for my mom has made me petty and mean. God has gotten my attention, Bob. I'm sorry."

"No need for an apology," Bob said. "I was a jerk when we were both at GCC. My grief was no excuse for treating you and your mother the way I did after she turned me down for a date." After taking a drink from his wine, he continued. "And as for me being religious, I'm not sure that fits either. I have faith, but it's taken a hit since my wife died. I talked to my pastor a lot back then, though it might be fair to say I *ranted* at my pastor in our sessions. He let me vent for hours, and I finally made my peace with God. I send prayers of gratitude each night for His wisdom and kindness."

"Thanks for telling me all that. I've been feeling distant from God lately, also. I love Mike so much, and I love Sophie too. But that kid knows how to press my buttons. Mike says I'm just exhausted."

"How is it for you when he says that?"

Kristen laughed. "Good counselor response, Bob. You get it, I can tell. I feel dismissed, even though Mike is right. I'm tired to the bone. A full-time job, a husband with a demanding career of his own, two kids, one a toddler and one full of emerging hormones, are testing my abilities big-time."

Kaye called Kristen over to help with cleanup, and after hugging her soon-to-be stepfather, she left for the kitchen. Louis settled in Kristen's empty chair.

"How was she, Bob? You two looked cozy, but I wanted to know if you needed support. Kristen's been tough lately."

"She's fine," Bob answered. "More to the point, how are you, Louis?"

"I'm good. Glad to see the end of the semester coming." Louis squirmed in his seat. "Katie and I are getting closer."

Seeming to enjoy his new role as patriarch, Bob smiled. "I'd say close is a good descriptor. You two have what I used to call 'googly eyes' when you look at each other."

The two men chuckled. "Yes, there's lots of that lately," Louis said. "Katie and I have decided we love each other, but it's still early. What about you and Kaye? You're engaged, right?"

"That we are," Bob said. "But I have some things to wrap up before we make an official announcement. What do you know about women's jewelry?"

"Not much. I know in the rarefied European circles I used to run with, the ring was often a competitive piece, not a token of love. The women would compare sizes of their gemstones, whether the ring was a family heirloom, which jeweler had done the work, and so on. The men would ridicule their women, but they reveled in the competition just as fiercely."

Bob blew out a frustrated sigh. "Why can't anything be simple?"

After everyone had left, Kaye and Bob enjoyed their coffee by the fire. Bob looked tired and worried, lines etching his forehead.

"What's wrong, honey?" Kaye asked. "Was Kristen hostile again? Did Louis put you on the spot? I saw you talking to both of them for a while."

"No, we had good conversations," Bob said. "In fact, I felt welcomed into your life by both of them."

"Then what is it? There's something on your

mind."

"I want us to be properly engaged," Bob said. "We need to talk about jewelry. It's important that I do this right, Kaye."

Kaye laughed and kissed the top of his head. "Bob, if we love each other without reservation, then we're doing it right. Couples have been getting engaged for centuries without jewelry."

Sensing his doubt, she added, "Here's the thing. I don't need an engagement ring at all. And a simple band will suffice when we marry. I have these gnarly arthritic fingers; there's no need for two rings that will turn the wrong way all the time."

"Did Stan get you an engagement ring?"

Kaye smiled at the memory. "He sure did. We had no money, no possessions, and a shabby furnished apartment when we got engaged. But he insisted on getting a line of credit with the local jeweler and bought me a precious one-fifth carat diamond solitaire. That little rock looked like the Hope diamond to me, but our parents were livid, calling it a waste of money. They told us we were irresponsible and not nearly ready to marry."

"I'm sorry," Bob said. "That's a painful memory."

"No, it's not," Kaye replied, still smiling. "In a way, it deepened my bond with Stan. He knew I loved jewelry and therefore, I was to have a diamond engagement ring."

"I'll bet you still love jewelry," Bob said. "You wear all kinds of pretty necklaces and doodads."

Kaye threw back her head and chortled. "True enough, Bob. But my costume jewelry is inexpensive and fun."

"Still, it's important that you have a piece of jewelry from me, and not one that's just for fun. Do you want to come shopping with me this weekend?"

Kaye reflected and again saw the worry in his eyes. "Honey, if I come, you'll do everything in your power to please me." She thought for a second and continued. "Which isn't necessarily a bad thing, but I want you to buy what you're comfortable with. I don't want to interfere. Does that make sense?"

"Only if you promise we can return whatever I pick for something you really like. Kaye, this is important. You seem to think it's no big deal to select wedding jewelry."

"Let's just say Rose's visit reminded me of what *is* a big deal," she said. "The big deal with love is the person, not the sparkle."

"So now I don't sparkle!" Bob wailed.

"Stop it!" Kaye said with a laugh. "As a matter of fact, I've been thinking. To keep costs in line, and to show you how much I love you, what if you had my original stone reset into a new ring? My girls would love that."

Kaye could see that Bob did *not* love the idea. He frowned, then sighed, then glared at her.

"Who said we have to keep costs in line? I can afford a proper ring for my intended."

"I'll give you the ring I got from Stan and you and the jeweler can work it out. If you'd rather not use the stone, that's okay."

"Deal," Bob said. "And in case you're wondering, I never wore a ring in my first marriage. I'm one of those guys who doesn't like to fiddle with jewelry. So, you're off the hook."

Kaye smiled. "But you're not off the hook, my dear. You *will* be wearing a ring after we marry, make no mistake about it."

The weekend came and Bob explained his jewelry dilemma to Louis. The younger man agreed to accompany Bob to the local jeweler. Bob knew Louis was on a personal fact-finding mission of his own. He and Katie weren't engaged yet, but Bob thought it would happen soon.

They got lucky with a good salesperson. Danielle, the daughter of the owner, listened carefully to Bob's complicated list of needs. "My fiancée only wants one ring. She doesn't want one that will twist and show the wrong side up. I've also got her first diamond, which she would be interested in having as part of the ring I give her. But I want to dazzle her." He shrugged and said, "Sounds tough to me."

Danielle flashed a perfect set of dental veneers. "Of course, you should dazzle the woman you love! It won't be tough at all, Bob. Come with me."

She led Bob and Louis to a case of wedding bands. "See these circles of diamonds? They're the same all the way around, which eliminates the 'right side up' problem of a half band." She sorted through several trays until she found the circlet she wanted. "This would be perfect for you. Each diamond is about one-fifth of a carat, like the stone you brought in, with a total of fourteen stones. The band would add up to just under three carats. Not too shabby, believe me. Her hand would sparkle like crazy."

"How much?" Bob asked, after telling Danielle Kaye's ring size and metal preference. He didn't feel like negotiating. He just wanted a great ring for Kaye, and this one fit the bill.

Quoting the base price, Danielle then adjusted it to having one diamond removed and Kaye's original diamond from Stan set in. "You know what else we could do? I could have our jeweler style the under gallery of your beloved's original stone with a tiny diamond. That would signal the original diamond's location. What do you think?"

Bob put his arm on Louis, who had seemed a little shaky since the price quote. "Great idea. Could the jeweler also fashion a tiny 'S' for Kaye's first husband? That would mean the world to her."

Arrangements were made for Bob to pick up the ring next week. The two men left the store and Bob looked at Louis.

"Are you okay? You looked a little queasy in there."

Louis gulped. "Let's get some lunch. I need food to settle my nerves. The cost of the ring you just bought almost amounts to the money I get for teaching half the academic semester. How am I ever going to afford getting engaged to Katie?"

Bob patted Louis on the back. "Lunch is on me, pal. You've got to start saving your money. And we'll talk about the differences between a first marriage and the second."

Louis still looked green. After they were seated at a nearby chain bar and food restaurant, with no complaints from the culinary arts professor, Bob tried to shore up Louis' confidence. "You heard Danielle. She educated us about the different quality diamonds. I chose the best I could afford for Kaye. And I'm sure you'll do the same for Katie, if that's what she wants. Remember, Kaye gave me the go-ahead to get what I thought was best. Katie will probably want to shop with you to select her ring."

"Good point," Louis said. "Knowing Katie, she'll grill the salesperson until they agree to let her have what she wants for 90 percent off." He sipped his beer and added, "I can only hope."

Chapter Fourteen

Louis had planned a quiet dinner on Sunday evening for he and Katie. She blew into his kitchen without knocking at his door. In contrast to the relaxed, rumpled look he loved, she looked tense and frazzled.

"What's wrong? You look like you could pound this round steak into submission for me." He handed her the meat mallet, and she took it, slamming the meat into a flat, tender mass.

"Sophie is what's wrong," Katie said. "At Kristen's request, I took her shopping for Christmas presents for her siblings. Michelle was easy, since she's a toddler. We could wrap up a shoebox and she'd have fun with it. But Sophie's brother in Indy, Anita's son, is almost five, which should still be easy, right?"

Louis nodded, having no idea what five-year-old boys liked in terms of toys. All he remembered was playing in the dirt, getting filthy, and enjoying it immensely. Of course, his mud pies had been the start of his career as a chef.

"But no! Sophie discounted everything I pointed out. She seemed determined not to buy him anything."

"What did you do?" Louis asked, taking Katie into his arms.

"I kept my cool, believe it or not, and said I had to get to your place for dinner. I think Kristen set me up."

"Or maybe she just couldn't deal with Sophie today. You're a good sister, Katie. And you've just had a first-hand glimpse of what Kristen's been going through." He stirred the French onion soup and poured Katie a glass of wine. "I don't know much about all this family stuff, but shouldn't Mike be taking Sophie out to buy things for Anita's kid?"

Katie kissed him soundly. "Excellent point, Louis. He should. No wonder Kristen always looks on guard. She never knows what's coming."

"And Sophie is smart enough to know her dad's handing her off," Louis added. "If you want to talk to Kristen about a do-over, I'd be glad to come with you."

That offer earned him another kiss, which was almost enough to keep the soup on simmer for a while. But he was hungry, and Katie needed to eat. "I'll broil the cheese topping for the soup if you dish up the salad," he said. "No more talk of others while we eat this gourmet dinner. The round steak is for later this week," he said as he placed the flattened mass in the refrigerator. "For now, we have issues of our own to discuss."

"What issues?" Katie said after the first slurp of her soup. "I thought things were going well after Mom's impromptu dinner. You're practically a member of my family."

"Exactly. I even went ring shopping with Bob yesterday. Your mom will be pleased, I think. But it started me worrying. I'm so used to the inherited jewels of the upper class in England that I had no idea what rings cost. Katie, I want you to have a nice ring, but I'm on a budget."

Katie grinned. "Welcome to the USA, land of working-class struggles," she said. "Louis, I'm pretty easy to please. I'm also delighted to hear we're engaged. You've never asked me to marry you!"

"I haven't? We said we love each other. The engagement is implied."

"No, not really. But I accept. I want to marry you, Louis," Katie said. "Very much."

Dinner was forgotten for a few minutes. Several kisses later, Louis dished up the soup, and dreamy, rumpled Katie came back to the present. "You don't talk much about your time in England. What should I know about your previous love?"

"The duchess was a good woman, but a product of her upbringing. Marrying well was her main focus. I was arm candy, mostly. She knew I didn't have the means to support her the way she wanted. Actually, she texted last week that she's engaged to a sixty-five-year-old owner of a brewery. You'd know the name if I told you. His family is absolutely furious."

"Are you furious? Or jealous? Or heartbroken?" Katie looked distinctly anxious.

"None of the above," Louis answered. "I'm pleased for Marie-Christine. She seems happy. More significantly, she seems relieved."

They cleaned the table in silence. Worried that Katie was in a funk about his lack of romantic proposal and about his history in Europe, he started a fire where they sat on the floor pillows. Katie started to relax again.

"Back to the important issue at hand," he said.

"What kind of rings do you like? I have new expertise on the subject, but not a lot of money to add to it."

Katie nestled into his arms. "I don't really know. Kristen got a yellow diamond when she and Mike were in the Caymans. Mom had a traditional stone from Dad. My friends run the gamut from huge diamonds, to colored stones, to simple wedding rings. I guess I would like an engagement ring, but something nontraditional. Like me."

"Like you," Louis repeated. "I agree. No run-of-the-mill ring for Katie Anderson."

Katie sat straight up. "We're forgetting your parents! I can tell my family easily enough that we're engaged, but we need to tell the Massons. Do you think they'll be upset?"

"Hardly. Both of my parents know much more about you than you'd expect. I've been calling them almost every night, to 'check in.' It only took my mom three days before she knew I was crazy about you."

He kissed Katie again and was about to lose his train of thought when she put a stop to his efforts. "Enough funny business, Louis. Do you mean you've been crazy about me for a while?"

"Well, you've driven me crazy since the first day we met," he admitted. "My mother knew it was more than just frustration with your approach to student internships. After a while I quit venting about you and began telling her about our dates, the Christmas cookie contest, and your mother's accident. Finally, my father called me out and asked when I was going to bring you back to their house as a member of the Masson family."

"Wow, everyone knew you were serious except for

me," Katie marveled. "I just figured we were going to have a fling and you'd move on to someone else."

"Never, Katie. I'm a one-woman man. Even with the duchess, I was completely faithful." He stared into the fire and added, "She was not."

"I'm sorry, Louis. For the record, I'm a one-man woman. You're it for me. If you ever dump me, I'm headed to the convent."

"They would never have you, Katie," he said with a wicked smile. "Lucky for me."

They cleaned the rest of the kitchen in quiet camaraderie. "Let's talk about Sophie's shopping expedition. Is she available some night this coming week?"

"Yep, Kristen said Sophie's here through the holidays. Anita and her family are going to be out of state. Which probably explains Sophie's attitude."

"Let's plan on Tuesday evening, then. You and I can do our jewelry shopping later in the week."

"Are you sure about that?" Katie asked. "I can wait if you need a few months after the holidays to shore up your checking account."

"No, I'm ready. As Bob said about Kaye, I want to do this properly. We'll set a budget and do some exploring to see what kind of microscopic diamond I can afford."

"It will be fine," Katie assured him. "You're engaged to the world's best bargain hunter."

Sophie sat in the back seat, sullen and feigning boredom. Katie tried to lighten the mood, asking about the Christmas program at her school, her recent indoor soccer matches, and her favorite classes. Nothing worked. Louis glanced and shook his head imperceptibly.

Okay, mister. You can deal with Little Miss Moody. Good luck.

They arrived at Gordon's only big-box store, and Sophie hunched down in the seat. "There's nothing but junk here. Why bother? My twerp brother has everything he wants anyway. Let's just get him a gift card and go get a burger."

"I need a few things from the grocery side of the store," Louis said mildly. He led them to the produce and dairy sections, placing his items in the huge cart. The trek across the expanse of the store seemed to relax Sophie.

"Now we can work on our problem. What do you buy a brother who needs nothing? What message do you want to send, Sophie?"

"No message. I barely know him," she muttered.

"Maybe you could send that message."

"What are you talking about?"

"Your gift could be something you could do together, so the two of you could get closer. I know that's a tall order, though. You may not be able to think of anything."

Katie looked away and smiled. Louis had a tricky streak she'd have to watch out for. She wondered if Sophie would fall for it.

"Who said I wanted to get to know my stupid brother better? I just need something to put under the tree. We're going to unwrap gifts when they all get back from my stepdad's family in Ohio."

"So not clothes, right? What about books? DVDs? An Indianapolis Colts jersey? What gets your brother pumped?"

Sophie looked at Louis, unwilling to engage, but

obviously hungry for the promised burger. "He likes the Pacers. He's tall for his age, they say. Who can tell what's tall for a five-year-old kid?"

"Ah, basketball. Now we're ready to shop." Louis steered Sophie to the sports section of the store while Katie followed. She knew Sophie was famished and ready to get to the restaurant. But to Louis' credit, they would leave with a gift. Kudos to her fiancé.

After checking out with Louis' groceries and a child-size Pacers jersey, they walked to the car. Katie also resolved to tell Kristen about Sophie's feelings of being left out, shunted from one home to another, and her pain at not truly belonging anywhere. Maybe Katie was making too much of it, but Sophie was hurting, and Kristen, Mike, and Anita needed to attend to it. Anita's husband, Grant, was a good stepdad, but clueless about Sophie. He needed to be on the team too. She said a quick prayer for the extended Sutliff family, and thanked God Louis didn't have any kids. Katie wanted children, but not for a while. Louis was all she could deal with at present.

Three days later, Louis arrived at Katie's home for their ring shopping date. She answered the door and led him to her office.

"What are we doing here?" he asked. "We need to go to the jeweler's and badger Danielle into selling us something you like and that I can afford."

"We'll get to that, silly. First, we do reconnaissance online, so we know what prices are like. I've decided I like cognac diamonds. They're elegant and remind me I'm marrying a gourmet chef."

Katie navigated search engines and sites like a pro. Together they settled on a style—a cognac solitaire encircled by small, white diamonds. The price on a bargain jewelry site, to Louis' surprise, was under his budget.

"Are you sure you like this, Katie? We can go for white diamonds if you want."

"No, I love this style. The cognac stone glimmers with different colors depending on the light. See? This picture reflects gold, honey brown, and even a little pink. It's perfect."

After Katie printed out the picture of the ring she wanted, they headed for Danielle's store. Louis introduced the two women, and they began his dreaded task. Finding a ring Katie would enjoy while he could still see his bank balance seemed impossible.

Danielle studied the photo Katie had printed. "This is lovely, Katie. It suits your personality. Solid, but a bit mercurial. We have some loose cognac stones in our vault. I'll be right back."

There were several stones to choose from. Katie decided on a one-carat round stone in a middling cognac color. Danielle quoted them a price for the stone and setting. Louis was breathing easier. Then Danielle added, "If you look closely, the ring in your photo has grayish, cloudy diamonds circling the main stone. I can set better diamonds into your ring, if you'd like. The price would go up, naturally."

Here it comes, Louis thought. *Surely, she doesn't think I'm in the same league as Bob, the retiree with a healthy pension and modest lifestyle.* Danielle then quoted a price only a few hundred dollars above Louis' budget.

He looked at Katie, who was beaming. He could handle a few extra bucks, if only to have seen that happy face this one time. Smiling at Danielle, he said, "It's a deal. Thanks for your help, Danielle. You've steered us well. When can I pick the ring up?"

New Year's Eve played out in the typical Anderson family tradition. Kaye cooked appetizers of all sorts, her children and their beloveds came over until about ten o'clock, and Bob enjoyed the chaos caused by Sophie and Michelle. The Sutliffs exited as Michelle started to fuss in earnest, and Katie helped her mother clean up the scattered food bits and shredded paper napkins.

Katie studied Louis. "Is everything all right? You were having a good time, but after Kristen and her tribe left, you got a little quiet."

"Nothing is wrong," he answered. "I just want to bring in the New Year on our own. I don't know if your mom and Bob expect us to stay until midnight."

"No worries. My hunch is that they want to greet the New Year on their own, too."

They left to a chorus of good wishes for the new year, and Louis pulled into Katie's drive. "Let's have a drink and have our own celebration."

Katie fidgeted as she unlocked her door. "Louis, I'm sorry. I have zero alcohol in the house. I thought we'd be at Mom's for a while longer."

Retrieving a bag from his trunk, Louis smiled. "I brought the goods," he said. "Guess what we're drinking."

Katie wondered what had gotten into him. He still seemed edgy, and there was no reason for it. "I have no clue, Louis. Maybe a new French wine you've discovered? Or that new bourbon from Kentucky?"

Louis shook his head and lofted a bottle of cognac. "This is our drink from now on," he said. "We'll relax and sip it by the fire as the clock counts down."

As the fire began to burn fully, Katie snuggled with Louis, pleased that he was calm at last. Her family, small as it was, could be a bit much. She hoped he'd adjust. Suddenly he rose and went on one knee. She stared at him, puzzled. "Louis, we're already engaged, remember?"

"Not officially. As you pointed out, I never really asked you to marry me. But now is the time. As we enter a new year, let's do it together. Katie Anderson, will you marry me? Will you promise to love, cherish, and obey?"

The glint in his eyes gave Louis away. Katie laughed and said, "Love and cherish are on the list, but 'obey' must be mutual if it's part of our vows. And if we're both obeying, nothing will ever be resolved." She kissed him with soft passion and added, "Yes, I'll marry you. I can't wait."

Louis rolled back into a sitting position and fished the ring box out of his pocket. "This will seal the deal," he said as he slipped the ring on Katie's finger.

"It's gorgeous!" Katie breathed. "Danielle was right. The better diamonds around the cognac stone set it off perfectly. I love you, Louis."

"And I love you, Katie."

Katie had a pang of worry. "Are you sure the ring didn't stretch your finances too much? I can pitch in if you want."

Louis laughed. "I've been eating cheese and peanut butter crackers for a couple of weeks now for lunch, and sometimes dinner. It's all good."

Knowing he was teasing, but still appalled that Louis would deign to eat such processed food even once, she gave him a playful punch. He answered with a not-so-playful kiss. Yes, it was all good.

At that point, the ball on the television began to descend. The new year was shaping up to be fabulous. Katie was happy in a way she'd never thought possible. It was all good, but more important, God was indeed good. She had to remember it more often.

New Year's Day was crisp and clear. Louis called Katie at eleven and suggested brunch in Indianapolis.

"Sounds lovely," she said. "But it will take an hour to get there, and unless you have reservations, we'll be waiting another hour for a table."

"No wait at all, and yes, I have reservations of a sort. We're going to my parents' place."

Katie wondered about starting the new year with a surprise for her potential in-laws. What if they didn't approve? She'd met them a few months ago, and they'd seemed like good folks. But Louis was their pride and joy, fresh from the sophisticated atmosphere of Europe. She was just an Indiana girl, hustling in her first job after her master's degree.

After a quiet drive, Louis pulled up in front of his parents' home. "It will be fine, Katie. I told you they've heard a blow-by-blow of our courtship. They knew right away that I was taken with you."

"But this is real, not some conjecture over the phone when you've had a good day fighting with me about your students," Katie grumbled. "I'm no duchess."

Brad and Evelyn Masson stepped out to the front porch with huge smiles on their faces. "Get in here, you two," Brad said. "It's barely twenty degrees outside, so we've got a fire going. And I'm hungry!"

Evelyn had the feast warm and ready to eat. Katie shut her eyes at the rich, creamy French toast. "How did you do this, Evelyn? This isn't like any French toast I've ever eaten." "It's stuffed challah bread, using whipped cream cheese and half-and-half instead of milk," she answered. "We also have an egg casserole if you'd like."

Hungry and eager to please, Katie nodded. "I'll have some of everything, if you promise to give me your recipes." She glanced and smiled at Louis. "I'm sure you've heard that I'm no rock star in the kitchen."

Brad laughed. "Everyone has to learn new skills sometime. Cooking is a skill." His eyes twinkled, much like his son's when teasing was about to happen. "The story I like best is when you fainted at the film of beef being butchered."

Evelyn poked Brad's chest. "Be nice, Bradley. Katie is a woman who feels things deeply, I can tell."

"She sure does," Louis agreed.

Katie laughed. Louis' parents were fun, sweet, and seemed to accept her for herself. What more could you ask for when it came to in-laws? "Yes, your son saved me after I almost did a full-on faceplant. My idea of fresh meat is the stuff you get at Kroger."

After eating and cleaning up, they took their coffees to the living room. Louis cleared his throat and announced their engagement. Brad and Evelyn were obviously in on the secret but made enthusiastic comments about Katie's ring.

"So, when's the date?" Evelyn asked. "It's January first. They say weddings take at least a year to plan, what with the dress, venue, entertainment, and food."

Katie looked up in horror. "We haven't set a date," she said. "And I can't imagine a Gordon wedding would take a year to plan. Most of my friends were married within six months of getting their rings."

"Well, you want to do it right," the older woman said. "I'd love to have your mom's contact information so that I can help with all the details."

I *knew it,* Katie thought. Evelyn wanted Louis to have a wedding worthy of a duchess. Katie was definitely not the aristocratic type. Feeling sated from the food, and a little hungover from the evening before, she added fuel to the fire. "The dress won't be an issue, Evelyn. I have a counselor friend who designs and fashions gowns as her side hustle. Lauren does beautiful work."

Louis grinned. "Mom, I'm sure Katie will find the perfect dress. The important thing is that we'll be married. I'm thinking that instead of you taking Mrs. Anderson's contact info, we should have you and Katie's family for dinner soon. It's easier to talk about details in person."

Smiling faintly, Evelyn nodded her head. Cutting in, Brad said, "Great thought, Louis. I'll bring the salad, as usual." Leaning toward Katie, he whispered, "Best layered salad ever. Louis says I use too much mayonnaise, but what does he know?" They all laughed. Louis a little less than the others.

On the drive back to Gordon, Katie did a status check with her soon-to-be husband. "So, what do you think? Will I measure up with your mom? Your father seems to like me well enough, but Evelyn wants you to have a wedding worthy of *People* magazine."

"No, she was testing you a bit," Louis said. "She and Dad met the duchess once when they came to visit me in England. I remember my mom saying Marie-Christine was the snottiest person she'd ever encountered. And those were her exact words."

Katie hoped Louis was right. If not, she'd get through it. She'd do anything to marry Louis. He loved her and she loved him. She was a lucky woman.

Chapter Fifteen

Kaye was humming. She remembered Stan teasing her about the habit, saying it meant he wasn't in the doghouse for a change. Despite his poor joke, they'd had a fine marriage. Stan hadn't been in the doghouse much, but he could feel Kaye's temper at times. She asked God for absolution for the times she'd failed Stan but held comfort in their happy last days together. In a way it was a blessing the heart attack had taken him suddenly. They'd been relaxed and focused on their kids, friends, and settling into retirement. Stan's final few years after his cancer treatment ended had been full of joy for both of them.

Now she hummed a *lot*. Her relationship with Bob made her supremely happy. He was also a good man, frustrated with aging, but willing to make changes to improve his health. His example worked for her, too. She'd been consuming more foods with calcium and was faithful with taking her osteoporosis medication.

More to the point, she was able to be as open with

Bob as she had been with Stan. She'd read books about the trials of emotional intimacy in second marriages (there seemed to be no reported trouble with the physical part!), but she and Bob confided everything to each other. Would it last? Would they eventually become complacent, taking each other for granted? She prayed not.

Well, so far, she didn't feel the least bit taken for granted. After the family had left on New Year's Eve, Bob presented her with a gorgeous engagement/wedding ring. He had been sweating a little, shy and nervous about whether he'd met her specifications.

"It's only one ring, Kaye, like you said you wanted. And it's the same all around, so if it twists, there's no wrong side."

At that point, she'd kissed him and said it was perfect.

"No wait, there's more," he'd replied, sounding like an infomercial. "Look at the inside. The little *s* and tiny diamond under one stone is marking where Stan's stone has been set. He'll always be with you, Kaye." He gulped and added, "Danielle worked hard with me on the design, but if it's not right, I have thirty days to return it and we'll look for something together."

Kaye laughed and said, "Never! Bob Benson, I'd never return such an artistic ring, full of love and care. I never thought such a ring was possible." She kissed him again and paused. "I do have one worry, though. This is what my girls call a 'bling-bling' ring. Can you afford this? And since we're in this together, can *we* afford it?"

"I can certainly afford it," Bob replied. "Louis almost had a fainting spell, however. Academic chefs don't make much, especially at GCC. He was worried about what to buy Katie."

"They'll work it out," Kaye had said. "Katie's a practical girl. She'll be happy with a tiny stone or a simple metal band."

Humming at the memory of her own first engagement, and now ecstatic about her second, she was puzzled when her doorbell chimed. Puzzled, Kaye walked to answer it. Bob wasn't due for dinner until later. She knew Katie and Louis were in Indianapolis at his parents' home. Kristen and Mike were likely still in pajamas with their kids.

Rose Dolce stood, clasping a large platter of antipasto. "Happy New Year," she sang. "I wanted to bring you a New Year's gift before your day got too busy. Hopefully this will help feed any company you have coming today."

It was a new year, a new day, and Kaye hoped she was a new woman of sorts. She smiled at Rose and beckoned her in. Taking her coat first, then the platter, she motioned for Rose to sit.

"Happy New Year to you, too, old friend. Where's Jim?"

"You know that husband of mine," Rose grumbled. "He's all set for football games ad nauseum with my sons and son-in-law. I'll see him later tonight."

"Well, I'm glad to see you," Kaye said graciously. "What can I get you? Coffee, tea, bubbled water?"

Each woman chose a flavored tea from the full basket on Kaye's kitchen island. Back in their chairs, Rose launched into her little speech. It sounded rehearsed to Kaye.

"Kaye, thanks for seeing me today. I hated my words last time I was here. I'm not usually that unkind and judgmental."

Arching her brows, Kaye remained silent.

"Okay, maybe I can be a little much," Rose hedged. "Know that I was coming from a place of love. I want you to be happy after all the sadness you had with Stan." She sipped her tea, wincing at the heat. "I see Bob makes you happy. That's all that matters."

An apology from Rose Dolce was significant. Kaye was grateful and said so. After a quick hug, she said, "I am happy, Rose. Bob is a good fit. We're not 'nursing or pursing', but we do take care of each other. Between his diabetes and my fragile bones, we're a good team. Our purses are healthy, thanks be to God. So please don't worry, Rose."

"And the families approve?"

"They do indeed. Bob and I are going to Evansville soon to make it official with his daughters, but he's told them over the phone."

"What's needed to make it official?" Rose asked.

"They haven't met me, or seen the ring," Kaye explained.

Back to her former inquisitive self and eager to have the latest gossip for her friends, Rose brightened. "There's a ring?"

Kaye held out her left hand. The diamonds twinkled in the light of the Christmas tree. Kaye made sure to show Rose that they made a complete circle around her finger.

Rose was appropriately impressed. "It's beautiful, like you," she said. "Are you going to have only one ring?"

Kaye nodded and said, "I just love it."

"I agree. One ring is enough to keep track of at our age. And yours won't ever have a wrong side up." Rose pronounced this advantage as if no one had ever considered it. Kaye let it go.

As Rose left two hours later, Kaye reflected on the contradictions inherent in having long-term friends. Shared history was wonderful, but only if friends understood that change was inevitable. Change could occur in careers, spouses, children, or anything, really. Rose was getting on board, however slowly. Kaye wondered what changes Rose had experienced in her journey. From the outside looking in, Rose's life looked almost perfect, although she'd said earlier she was worried about Annie. But Kaye knew better than to assume perfection blessed anyone. God made our lives full of promise and wonder. He also gave us free will, the chance to make plenty of mistakes, and therefore an imperfect world.

She heard a knock at the door, followed by Bob's cheery greeting. "How's my best girl?" he asked. "Anything new since last night?"

After their hug and kiss, Kaye said, "Rose was here and approved of my new ring." Noting Bob's eye roll, she kissed his forehead and added, "She wanted to make amends, and she did. Rose even liked the idea of one ring instead of two! So, anything new with you?"

"Not much. I had good conversations with my girls, and we're set to visit them and their families the second weekend of this month." Bob seemed pensive. "They're bugging me about setting a date. I've been so preoccupied with getting engaged, I haven't thought about it."

"Then let's think about it," Kaye said. Pouring

them each a glass of tea, she pulled out her phone and began to swipe through the months on the calendar app. "Kristen said Sophie starts outdoor soccer in March, which will eat into her free time. She and Mike are making every effort to remind Sophie she's a true part of their family. Louis and Katie will have the busiest part of their semesters in April and May, with final exams mid-May. I guess we're looking at a summer wedding."

"What are your thoughts about that?" Bob asked, using his new cautious counseling technique.

"I guess it's fine. But doesn't it seem far away? It's January first and we're talking about marrying in June at the earliest."

"Agreed. What about before March? Later this month or February?"

Kaye smirked. "We could really go for sentimentality and have our ceremony on Valentine's Day. Why not?" She drummed her fingers on her glass. "Everyone goes out that evening, so the restaurants are already booked. But I bet we could reserve the Gordon Park clubhouse for the ceremony and reception. Kristen's friend Reverend Taylor would be happy to help; even if he can't marry us, he'll know someone who can. Unless you've got a minister in mind, that is. I don't mean to presume or take control. It's your wedding, too."

"No, I'm between churches at the moment," Bob admitted. "In fact, I was never much into church. After my wife died, I was pretty mad at God. You saw some evidence of that in my disregard for your grief over Stan and my callous treatment of Kristen. I haven't been back to church since the funeral."

"Well, it's time, Bob. At this point in my life, I

realize I need to keep thanking God for my blessings along with asking for help with my health. Those are good things, but church attendance also reminds me to praise Him and to seek out ways to serve others."

"I understand. As somebody once said, 'Those blessed with the sweet wine of a long life must also expect to sample the dregs.' Being thankful will help me focus less on the constant state of hunger I'm in on this diabetic diet." He grinned. "One of my blessings will be my new wife, my companion on the journey."

"Bob, you're a glass half-empty kind of guy today. Where's your New Year's optimism? The more we lean on God, the better off we'll be."

The next weekend, Louis pulled out all the stops for what he was styling as a "meet and greet" for his parents and Kaye and Bob. He adjusted one of his favorite menus from the London restaurant, which included a salad featuring romaine lettuce, prosciutto and crème fraîche, grilled filets, garlic mashed potatoes, roasted asparagus, and crusty French bread. For dessert, he used his trusty ice cream maker to fashion both a coconut-lime sorbet and a pecan praline ice cream. The menu had a suitable Midwestern sensibility while also being a bit innovative. He was being judgmental and anxious at the same time. Hopefully the Massons and Kaye and Bob would get along just fine.

Finally, he acknowledged the truth. Katie had intuited his mother's push for a "proper" wedding. To Evelyn Masson, that meant pulling out all the stops, circa the 1970s—engraved invitations, numerous bridal showers, multiple attendants, and a lavish sit-down meal reception with a live band. Louis knew his mother would also ask for a newspaper announcement. The woman was so out of touch she didn't realize such things were mostly long gone. Gordon didn't even have a daily paper, just a thin biweekly affair that was out-of-date the minute it hit the shelves. Knowing Katie, she would have little patience with his mother's interference.

He admitted Katie and Evelyn shared some common characteristics. Both were perfectionists, each had a distinct individual style, and neither was shy about stating her opinion. Sending a silent prayer to the heavens, he asked God for tolerance all around.

Katie pushed open the door just as he finished setting the table. "I brought the wine as requested," she said. "Two whites and two reds. Good thing you wrote down the specifics. I'd never have remembered those fancy names."

Louis kissed her absently on the top of her head and she frowned. "What's wrong? You have that pained look you get when I rile you up about a student."

Laughing, he drew her near him for a proper kiss. "I guess you know me better than I thought. I really want tonight to go well. My mom can be a bit particular."

"I know. All I can say is I'll do my best to listen to Evelyn's desires for the wedding. My mother is pretty loose about it all, since she's absorbed in her own preparations. Maybe that will help."

"Fingers crossed," Louis said. "Let's open some wine and relax before the evening begins."

Three sips into their wine, the doorbell rang.

Both couples had arrived at once, so introductions were already made. Wine was distributed, to all except Kaye, who wasn't drinking due to her "bone issues." Everyone made nice chit-chat and after a few minutes, Louis called them to dinner.

The menu and quality of food were roundly praised. Coffee and frozen treats were taken in the living room. After her first bite of sorbet, Evelyn began. "This was just lovely, Louis. Kaye and Bob, it's been a treat to meet Katie's mom and soon-to-be stepfather. But now we must get to work. It's painfully obvious these two lovebirds are much too busy and stressed to plan a wedding." She smoothed her knife-creased slacks, adjusted her numerous bangle bracelets, and continued, "I'm more than happy to help. Katie, if you'll let me know your preferences—colors, flowers, menu for the reception, venue, and so on—I'll get right on it. And of course, you need to set a date. First things first."

Louis looked at Katie, who swallowed hard. Luckily, he was the only one who noticed. *God, please give her patience,* he prayed. *My mother is a good woman, but subtle as an erupting volcano.*

His prayer must have worked. Katie smiled at Evelyn, and it seemed genuine.

"Evelyn, you are too kind," she said. "I'm so grateful for your offer to help. I'm still getting used to my gorgeous ring, and too busy to even think of such things. Also, my priority is to help my mom with her own wedding. Then Louis and I will focus on what we want for our ceremony and celebration. It will all fall into place."

It was Evelyn's turn to swallow hard. "But don't you think it's a good idea to begin work on some of the tasks?" she asked. "My schedule is wide open."

Kaye jumped in. "Katie, I'm so glad to hear you say you'd like to help me. Bob and I were talking about a Valentine's Day wedding, which gives us very little time. Your assistance will be invaluable. And things will fall into place for you and Louis, as you said."

Determined not to be ignored, Evelyn veered to a different topic. "Well, you can't wait too long on the dress, Katie. They take a minimum of six months to arrive, more often, a year."

"Yes, remember Evelyn, I'm already planning my dress!" Katie said. "I've talked to Lauren and she's working up some designs for me." Detailing Lauren's side career as a dress designer, Katie told Evelyn about the history of the bridal gowns fashioned for the GCC women in Lauren's circle of friends. Katie pulled her phone from her pocket. "Let me show you the dresses she's done in the past. Here's my sister, Kristen, in hers. It was fashioned from Lauren's own gown but reworked to suit Kristen. What do you think?"

Evelyn viewed the tea-length, multicolored pastel tulle gown with wide eyes. "It's sure different, isn't it? Did Kristen have a Vegas wedding?"

Evelyn's query caused an audible inhale from Kaye, who became steely-eyed.

"My daughter did not wed in Vegas!" Kaye said. "She and Mike had the wedding of their dreams, which turned out to be a fall ceremony on the GCC campus. I've never been to a happier wedding. Several of my friends agreed with me afterward."

Louis glanced at Katie. Unlike her mother, so far she seemed calm.

"Evelyn, I can understand that Kristen's dress isn't for everyone. My style, for special occasions as well as every day, is more subtle. Tailored, minimalistic, you know? If you and Mom can come into the kitchen, I'll show you Lauren's sketch for my outfit. It's on my phone as well." She winked at Louis. "We can't have the groom seeing my gown before the big day."

Appeased, Evelyn went to the kitchen. Kaye held Katie's hand and whispered, "You're doing great," as they followed.

Once in the kitchen, they settled around Louis' dining nook table and Katie pulled up Lauren's rendering of her ideal wedding look. It was a two-piece dress of ivory silk crepe-de-chine. The A-line top had softly padded cap sleeves and ended just at the waistline, which was edged in a two-inch border of beaded lace. The skirt was softly gathered, with a high-low hem.

"Isn't it perfect?" Katie breathed. "I'll feel so feminine, but not overdone with lots of lace, tulle, and chiffon. No frills, but still elegant. And I'll be able to dance in comfort, since there's no long hem or train. What do you two think?"

Evelyn's silence spoke volumes. Katie's disdain for lace, tulle, and chiffon seemed to be a direct insult. Kaye spoke first to bridge the silence.

"It's you, honey," she said. "I agree completely. Are you going to have a veil or headpiece?"

"No, maybe a satin headband in the same beaded lace as the top. We'll see."

"No veil," Evelyn whispered. "No gown. No train. It's not a wedding gown at all."

Leaving Bob and Bradley to their discussion of

basketball rankings, Louis peeked into the kitchen in time to hear Evelyn's statement and notice Katie's thunderous look. She'd had enough of his mother. Understandably so.

"Hey, ladies, enough hogging the kitchen. I need to retrieve more coffee."

"Sounds wonderful," Katie said. She hugged him and focused on his mother.

"Evelyn, I will need your help with one thing right away."

Startled, Evelyn said, "Sure, anything."

"We need to meet for a girls' lunch so you can give me all of Louis' favorite recipes. Not his gourmet, fancy ones, but the food he grew up with. I figure he got his love for cooking from you. I need to be able to prepare those dishes."

Smiling, Evelyn seemed mollified. "How's next week for you, Katie? I'm pretty much free whenever your schedule allows."

The evening grew more relaxed and everyone enjoyed their coffee. After the two couples were on their way, Louis pulled Katie to him. "You are a saint, my love. You'll soon get to know my mom and realize she just wants the best for her only child. There's no doubt in my mind you're the best for me. She'll get it, trust me."

"What about her wish for a royal wedding in Indiana?" Katie groused.

"She'll adjust. It might help if you scour the wedding blogs and online videos. I'll bet you can find some aristocratic European bride with a dress like yours."

Katie pulled away. "How much did you see?"

"I saw nothing on your phone," Louis insisted. "I

did see my mother's face, however. Your dress isn't traditional, I take it?"

"Depends on your idea of traditional," Katie hedged. "Fine. It's a little different but it suits me. You'll love it. I even show a little midriff."

"You're right. You won't look like a meringue and you'll be showing some skin. I already love it."

Epilogue

Valentine's Day was cold—really cold. Kaye thanked her lucky stars (and God) that she and Bob had been able to secure the clubhouse for their ceremony. She was also happy in her choice of attire, a dusty pink brocade pantsuit with a soft jacket embellished with glittering rhinestone buttons. Bob was to wear his best suit, which thanks to his recent healthy eating, fit him perfectly.

Her girls were to read the scripture selections. Reverend Taylor approved their nontraditional choices, which focused on God's love for all, even the woman from Samaria. Bob had won a minor victory, though.

"Yes, John, Chapter Four is good, honey," he'd said. "But I'm glad we included the verse from Song of Solomon," Bob said. "It's important to address the passion of the happy couple."

Kaye had blushed, surprised this man could still make her heart flutter. She pinned on her corsage just as her daughters entered the room adjacent to the gathering area.

"The place looks grand, Mom," Kristen said. "The flowers, the canopy, and the rented chair coverings are just beautiful. How are you doing?"

"I'm fine," Kaye said. And she was. Marrying Bob was what she wanted. They would be each other's "nurse and purse" for as many years as God allowed. Even that cranky Rose Dolce had come around. Sure, the dazzling diamond ring had started the process, but she'd admitted to Kaye that she was a little envious of the intense love between Kaye and Bob.

The GCC string quartet began their gentle music. Katie kissed her mother. "Mom, you're lovely. That suit is perfect for you. Get out there and marry Bob Benson before he strokes out. He's so nervous, Louis had to give him a nip of sherry from the reception bar."

And so, the wedding commenced. The music, the verses, and the kind words from Reverend Taylor were all perfect. Kaye had a flash of her first wedding at age twenty-one, when she was full of nerves and afraid she was making a huge mistake. She hadn't made a mistake then, and she wasn't making one now. Bob was perfect for her, just as Stan had been. *Thank you, Lord.*

The reception was in full swing. Katie and Louis sat alone, discussing their own wedding, to be held early in the summer.

"Let's talk about reception food," Katie said, as she licked the buttercream frosting from the wedding cake off her lips. "I'm thinking about having some authentic Midwestern cuisine. A buffet with beef sliders, loaded tater tots, fried macaroni and cheese, maybe with a veggie tray to satisfy the healthy eaters. And you know what would make an awesome wedding cake?"

Louis arched his brows. "No, darling, what? Perhaps a fondant four-tiered beauty with edible flowers?"

"Yuck," Katie replied. "I was thinking of a red velvet chocolate cake with cream cheese frosting. Wouldn't that be special?"

Louis kissed her tenderly and shook his head. "No, it would not. I can't choke down red food coloring in a chocolate cake, no matter how much I try to make it palatable." Ignoring her giggle, he scowled at Katie. "Here's how it's going to go—I let you decide on your dress and flowers, and you're going to let me be in charge of the food."

"Perfect," Katie said, planting a loud smooch on Louis' cheek. "Absolutely perfect."

Discussion Questions

1. Leaving a place doesn't change what is in our hearts and minds. Kaye's grief and move to Phoenix is an obvious example. What about Katie's move back to Gordon? And Louis' retreat from Europe to Indiana?

2. In addition to grief, Kaye is surprised to have to deal with forgiveness when she buys her new home. Did you trust Bob Benson's explanation for his past cruelty to Kristen?

3. Sophie Sutliff seems to have transformed from a sweet little girl to an annoying preteen. What would you tell Kristen and Katie as they interact with her? How do Sophie's behaviors reflect her inner turmoil?

4. Bob Benson's illness alienates Linda and causes Rose Dolce to warn Kaye off. What are your thoughts about caring for others who are not "family"?

5. Kaye disagrees with Bob's view on illness as punishment for past sins. What are your thoughts about health trials? How much responsibility do

we have for our poor health? Is there any way to know? What can we do to strengthen our faith during times of pain and suffering?

6. Kaye dislikes the meddling that sometimes occurs in small towns. What are the advantages of living in a small community? Can life in a big city provide those advantages?

7. What do you think of Kaye's worry that she and Bob are only one functioning person together? Don't couples always compensate for each other's weaknesses? Or is it different as we age and lose some of our abilities?

8. Kristen let her own problems cloud her view of Bob's suitability for her mother. How can a loving adult child balance concern for aging parents with their own life challenges?

9. Discussing the wedding with Louis' mother brought out some of Katie's insecurities. When did you experience such feelings—of being insecure, not enough, or inadequate?

10. Kaye isn't nervous as she prepares to marry Bob. How do you explain the difference from her first wedding to Stan?

Dear Friends,

Thank you for reading *Back Home for Love*. Romance readers, myself included, live for the happily-ever-after ending. The finale of the Indiana Romance series reminds us that an HEA will still include some bumps in the road—Kristen's challenging times with Sophie, Annie's battle with infertility, and Kaye's health issues. In all of our times like these, God is with us. Focusing on His presence helps us to remember we aren't alone, which for me, is one of the worst types of pain. As always, God comforts us when we most need Him.

Take good care,
Leanne

A Look At:
Home Is Where You Are

Rafter O Ranch Book One

by Natalie Bright & Denise McAllister

They say home is where the heart is...

But what if that home is located in a barren, unforgiving land with nothing but giant animals, wind, and unrelenting dirt?

When Nathan Olsen brings his wife and 8-month-old son home to the Rafter O ranch for his little brother's wedding, he only planned to be there for a few days. But, being home with his family again stirred up longings he never expected to have for the ranch, and the way of life that only a rancher with generations of family who worked the land could understand.

Indya Olsen agreed to head back to the barren land that his husband was from for just a long week-end. She preferred their new way of life in Santa Fe, New Mexico and didn't want to stay away a day longer.

But when the wedding turned into a disaster that required Nathan to stay and help, will more than their marriage survive the turmoil of a new birth, a heart attack, and severe jealousy that turned to hatred?

When the heart isn't where it wants to be, can a marriage survive? Can a large family survive the feud that so much change will bring?

With Nathan and Indya at odds, Indya soon discovers a warm and welcoming family who accepts a worldly island girl into their close-knit group, but it's not enough. Can this stark and barren landscape become a place she loves as much as her beloved Santa Fe? Is this rambunctious family and their troubles too much for a marriage to survive?

Rafter O is set in the same Texas town as Wild Cow Ranch. Pick up your copy today and jump into a cattle ranch with endearing and unforgettable characters.

COMING SOON

About the Author

After a satisfying career as a psychologist, Leanne Malloy focused her efforts on writing novels that reflect her firm belief in God's love, grace, and provision.

She and her husband live in Indiana and visit their daughter in South Carolina as often as possible.

A homebody at heart, her life is full as long as there are family and friends in frequent contact, opportunities to travel, and books to be written.